BOOK
OF
RULES

Noble
Press

ALSO BY GAIL NOBLE-SANDERSON

The Lavender House in Meuse
The Passage Home to Meuse
The Lavender Bees of Meuse

THE BOOK OF RULES is a series of documents that contain direct instructions for all railway employees conducting railway operations including engine drivers, firemen, brakemen, conductors, porters, clerical workers, porters, and administration. All employees operating the locomotives and trains (engineers, fireman, brakeman, conductors) must pass rigorous examinations covering all rules and regulations to ensure the safe operations of the trains.

This book is dedicated to my railroading father,
William Howard Noble, Jr.

TABLE OF CONTENTS

A NOTE FROM THE AUTHOR

Welcome to *The Book of Rules,* the first book of The Railway Mysteries series. I wanted to give you a little background as to why I would choose to write a novel in which the major characters are railway employees, and a good portion of the plot involves events occurring in the railway offices in the Swansea, Wales, railway station.

My father, William Howard Noble, Jr., was a railroad engineer in Ohio. He also served in the US Army during World War II, driving trains in Alaska. Following the war, he returned home to Ohio and resumed his civilian career as a railroad engineer. He worked for several different railroad lines, including the Baltimore and Ohio; Norfolk and Western; and the Akron, Canton and Youngstown. After the war, three of his brothers also worked during some part of their lives for the railroads, two of whom helped to lay new electrical lines after World War II, and the third also became an engineer. Their father, my grandfather William Howard Noble, Sr., was a train dispatcher for most of his working life. My mother, Kathryn Kunsman, along with my father's sister, Florence Noble, worked for the Akron, Canton and Youngstown Railroad as secretaries before my parents were married. This was a family who lived and breathed all things railroads. My father said when he wasn't driving an engine, he was dreaming he was.

Being born and raised in a railroading family provided my sister, brother, and I unique and interesting travel experiences. Beginning in elementary school, in the 1950s, and into my teenage years, my grandmother, Edith Kunsman, would take me and my sister, Kathy, on train trips throughout the continental United States. We traveled on the gloriously appointed passenger trains that traveled from the Eastern Seaboard to the Pacific. When we rode coach, Grandma Edith would pack us lunches in shoeboxes filled with her fried chicken, home-baked goods, and enough amazing food to last us two days.

When we traveled for longer than a day or two, she would book a sleeper car, and to me, that was luxury unsurpassed! We ate in the elegant diner cars, where the tables were set with crisp ironed linens and adorned with fresh flowers. The servers were gracious, and the choices on the menu were superb. Most meals you ate with fellow passengers who joined you at your table, and interesting conversations ensued. While we ate at our leisure, the stewards were busy making up our room for the night. When we returned to our cabin, the beds, usually a double on the bottom and a single overtop, were made up and turned down. I loved climbing into those cozy bunks, looking out the large windows after dark as towns whirled by. I fell fast asleep to the rocking of the train and the clacking of the metal wheels on the tracks.

This book series is to honor my railroading family, who instilled in me a lifelong love of train travel. As to why the stories are set in Wales, you would have to ask my characters, as they always choose the settings for my books. And now I love Wales as well! Happy reading and hop aboard a train.

CHAPTER 1

THE VICARAGE –
MONDAY, 28 OCTOBER 1946

The small house sat high atop a broad knoll, with an expansive view of the Bristol Channel to the south. This morning, an icy breeze was blowing off the sea. Moisture from last night's rain hung in the air, and leaves from the thick blanket on the ground clung to Drew's boots as she pushed the creaky white gate open with more force than intended. Sam had no business telling her to be realistic and not hope for the impossible! Her frustration played out with each fierce kick through the brilliantly colored offerings from the oaks and maples. He had no right to scoff at her ambition. What had she been thinking? If she was honest, she was most angry at herself for even sharing her dreams with anyone.

It was early still, the pale sun appearing listlessly through a break in the clouds as Drew walked through the vicarage's small garden to the front door. The church itself was set farther back on its own expanse of property, a pleasant walk between the two buildings. She knew the vicar would not have smoldered a fire in his front grate that she could cast a log onto and bring quickly to life. She stood in the cold, searching her brown leather satchel for the large key, finding it at the bottom. It turned easily in the old lock, and she opened the door.

Attempting to put her frustrations aside and get on with her day, Drew was greeted by the particular scent of the place. She knew all homes held lingering smells of the day-to-day events of those that lived there, and she was always surprised, even a little sad that the vicar's home was perpetually cold and smelled of nothing more than cleaning wax and regret. So different from her own home.

Drew loved the cottage she shared with her granda, Howard, and her nonna, Naomi. Her grandparents' home always greeted her with the aromas of her own life: cooking spices and pasta and Nonna's soft scent of lavender lingering in the air. In spring and summer, colorful flowers from their gardens stood tall and fragrant in the crystal vase placed in the center of the old pine kitchen table, scars worn smooth from the many meals and gatherings over the years. In autumn, the pungent scents from canning the garden's harvest filled the house. Smells of holiday baking and pine boughs enhanced the sense of warmth and security through the winter months.

But the long years of the Second World War had taken their toll. Seasons once marking the passage of time had been marred by news of battles and bombings, tragedy, loss and hardship, rations, and worry. Drew was looking forward to the holidays this winter, the first in many years that peace and renewal might be celebrated. It seemed a shame that the vicarage was such a desolate place of a home.

Drew had taken this early morning Monday through Thursday cleaning and light meal preparation at the vicarage to augment her salary at the railway station. The church didn't pay much, but the job didn't entail much, and in these war-torn days of continued rationing and recovery, it all helped. Arriving by seven, she was on her way by nine, where her responsibilities at the station awaited her. Neither job was overly demanding, and only one proved interesting and would hopefully be a steppingstone to the life she knew she was meant to live. But it was taking a long time and Drew was not a patient young woman.

As with every morning that she had been making the man his breakfast and lunch, feeding his cat and cleaning his rooms, the vicar was supposedly sound asleep in his bedroom. At least, that is what she was told by the Women's Church Auxiliary that hired her. She was to be as silent as possible and go about her duties as instructed and then quietly leave.

She had never formally met Vicar Hughes and had seen him only occasionally about town. Her family did not attend the Anglican church, and when they did go to services, it was the Catholic church they went to. Nonna insisted on it.

Drew sometimes passed the vicar on the road as she was cycling to and from the rail station in Swansea. The first few times she saw him, she would wave and call out a greeting, but he always had his eyes cast down to the road and never looked her way. Thereafter, she just passed him in silence. His person seemed much like his home: silent, sparse of spirit and empty of hope.

It was disconcerting to think the man was sleeping with no idea she was even in the house. His heavy door was always closed but sometimes she imagined she could hear him snoring. Most mornings, she heard nothing at all. This day would be no different than any other, except that Drew persisted in a rare foul mood, Sam's words still nipping at the edges of her thoughts.

She stepped across the threshold, shutting the door a bit too hard, and kicked her boots off. One hit the leg of a side table in the small front room and made a racket that woke the vicar's cat and brought it leaping from the sofa to see what the commotion was about. Drew cringed and stood perfectly still, fearing she had also woken the man. But the only sign of movement was his cat, now purring and rubbing itself round her legs. She had become attached to the very large, very orange tabby cat, the only life she ever saw in this old house that today smelled musty and stale.

Most mornings when she arrived the cat was sleeping, its more than generous length fully extended across the back of the sofa. It would wake and stretch itself when Drew came in, clawing the thick crocheted afghan of many-colored squares draped over the back, the single object of color in the room. Then it would yawn, sit up and give Drew a welcoming *meow* before jumping down to weave in and out between her long legs, begging for its breakfast. As was her habit, she scooped the furry beast into her arms and buried her face into its thick coat, her long copper curls shining against the cat's thick orange fur. Its motor roared as she leaned against the wall, wanting to stay here this day, safe and accepted by this warm soul who obviously enjoyed her company.

"At least you understand me, my friend." She set the animal on the floor, thinking as she often did that, although he was a large cat, both the thick woven collar round his neck and the large bell he wore seemed too heavy for the animal.

The sitting room was as sparsely furnished as the rest of the house. Besides the old couch and small table, two worn stuffed chairs sat on each side of the cold hearth. No rugs, nothing hanging on the walls, and only sad thin curtains hung from the window.

Drew entered the small kitchen and set her ever-present leather satchel on the floor by the table. Nothing looked touched since she had last been there. The cat followed close behind and waited for her to scoop food into its small glass dish and set it beside the matching one she had filled with fresh water. Not feeling her usual energetic self, Drew plopped down onto one of the two wooden chairs at the table and gazed out the kitchen window. The view looked out to the back of the house, where the garden had gone to wild from years of neglect after the gardener moved away during the war. She sighed, telling herself she would take a moment to think before sweeping the floors. The day was still dim, and she shivered in the cold gloom of the sad house.

CHAPTER 2

FOUL FINDINGS – THURSDAY, 31 OCTOBER

Monday evening, Mara Roberts, of the Women's Church Auxiliary, rang Drew at home, letting her know the vicar would be out of town the next two days and she need not return to the house till Thursday. With the passing of the days, most of her annoyance with Sam had faded, leaving her more than sad, more than angry—she felt bereft. She hated this. It made her feel out of control and lethargic, not her usual self at all. When Thursday came round, it brought much the same dreary, mist-filled weather as Monday, and Drew continued, as she had all week, to carry the weight of her frustration once again into the vicar's house.

She entered the vicarage and slipped off her short boots. It took a moment to realize that the cat was not there to greet her. Something seemed out of sorts. She walked the few steps from the front room into the kitchen and finally back to the vicar's study. Still no cat. But what *was* present was a terrible smell. A strong unfamiliar odor—ripe and rancid. Seeing no sign of the orange tabby, she began looking for the source of the putrid stench and found it strongest at the vicar's bedroom door.

I'll just open the door a crack, she thought. Maybe he's gone, and I can finally give the room a thorough cleaning. It does seem as it needs one. Or maybe he's sick and needs assistance. Maybe the cat is with him. Maybe I need to go get help.

Before she thought further, Drew slowly opened the door. The foul odor was overwhelming. She gagged violently and quickly covered her nose. Slowly she walked through the dim light and stood at the foot of the bed. Even in the thin light of morning she could see the blood that lay across the bed linens. Copious amounts of blood, now dried and brown against the stark white sheets. The vicar was lying on his back with open eyes staring up at the ceiling, a look of astonishment upon his face. The large open gash across his throat left no doubt as to how he had died, how he had been murdered.

She stood there motionless, feelings of disbelief ringing as alarms in her head. Her heart was racing. He must have been dead for days for him to smell so terrible. She had last been there on Monday and today was Thursday. She had never encountered a fresh, or not so fresh, dead body. With a last look at the man, she turned slowly and walked out of the bedroom, closing the door behind her.

She went directly to the phone on the side table. With trembling hands she dialed 999 and asked to be put through to the police. After what seemed several long minutes, someone answered. Drew realized she had been holding her breath and tried to calm herself before carefully telling the man what she found. In a stern voice, he told her the authorities would be there shortly, and she was not to leave until they arrived. And she was definitely not to touch anything.

Drew tried to prepare herself for questions the police were sure to ask, but her ears were ringing, and she could not stop the trembling in her limbs. She thought she might be sick. She attempted to recall anything unusual when she first walked into the house and then into the vicar's bedroom. She felt strangely detached and wondered at it.

She also wondered how the murderer had entered. Since the front door was locked when she arrived, they must have come in another way. She walked through the kitchen to the back door that led out to the garden at the rear of the house. It was ever so slightly ajar. The lock was tampered with, as though it had been forced open with a tool of some kind. How had she not noticed?

Hearing the doors of autos slam shut, she returned to the front door and looked through the window. Two cars were parked in the lane, and four men in uniform were coming through the gate. She held the door open for them.

"Where is the body, lass?" asked the first man through. Drew pointed to the closed door of the vicar's bedroom. Without so much as an acknowledgment, they all walked directly to the bedroom and slowly opened the door. One officer took out a notebook and pen while the one who appeared in charge began describing what could be seen from the doorway. A third got his camera ready and began photographing the scene.

Upon entering the room, they walked cautiously toward the dead man, then all stood silently looking down at the body. They spoke in quiet voices as the officer with the notebook wrote furiously.

Drew had seen enough. She took herself into the kitchen and sat at the table, waiting for the officers to question her. She was a voracious reader of crime and mystery novels and knew the officers always needed to question whoever found the body.

Three of the constables left the bedroom and each walked about the other small rooms of the house, from the sitting room into the bath, the study and finally the kitchen. The fourth one, apparently having finished his notes from the bedroom, joined the others silently looking round the kitchen.

One stepped to the back door, saying, "This door's been jimmied. This was the way in." After all four examined the damaged door and made their additional notes, they filed outside to the back garden.

Drew was puzzled. They still had not acknowledged that she was in the house, much less in the kitchen with them, and oddly, they did not seem interested in talking with her. When the officers returned, they formed a circle of sorts and again began talking with each other.

"Excuse me? I am wondering if you want to ask me any questions about finding the vicar this morning?"

"And you are?" asked the one in charge. All four stood looking at her as if she had suddenly appeared out of thin air.

"I am Drew Davies. I cleaned and cooked for Vicar Hughes four mornings a week. I was told he was going to be gone for a few days, that was on Monday, and I didn't need to come back until today, Thursday. So, I did. And when I arrived at seven this morning, I found him dead in his bed." The men again just stared at her as though she were an apparition speaking Latin.

Finally, the officer with the notebook nodded his head and asked, "When you arrived this morning, did you notice anything in the house was disturbed or missing? Was there anything out of the ordinary?"

"Well, of course, finding the Vicar Hughes murdered in his bed was out of the ordinary, but as far as I could tell, the other rooms in the house were undisturbed.

"Very well, Miss Davies. I wrote down your name, and if we need anything further from you, you will be contacted. You can go now." With that, they resumed their tight circle in the kitchen, listening to the one in charge.

Drew, completely befuddled at their curt dismissal of her, gathered her satchel and coat from the kitchen chair and walked slowly past them to the front door. She put on her boots and left, thinking how very horrible the morning had been. It was hard to believe the vicar was inside, dead under the horribly bloodied linens. She found her legs and arms were still shaking, her stomach still rolling as she walked carefully down the front steps, and decided to walk beside her bicycle until she felt steady enough to ride. She hoped by the time she arrived at the station she would have regained her wits enough to tell Granda about it all.

Once she reached the main road, she mounted her bicycle. She swung her right trousered leg over the crossbar, and her feet found the pedals as she pulled out onto the Mumbles Road along Swansea Bay to the train station. She pedaled as quickly as her shocked state allowed and suddenly found herself wondering what had happened to the cat. She decided she would go back later to find it.

The Swansea railway office was a long, windowed room opposite the station's entrance. Four marred wooden desks looked out at the passenger waiting area. Her granda's desk was on the left and Drew's a foot apart to the right. Behind him sat Fitzhugh, and behind her, a desk that was used by various railwaymen as needed. Out in the lobby, a bank of metal lockers lined the wall beside the main double-door entrance. To the left, the barred ticket window stood sentry as the passengers departed and arrived through the adjacent doors to the platform and the double set of tracks.

The tracks were empty now, with only a few freight cars on the siding, waiting to be coupled onto the train arriving later in the day. With no passengers about, it was a good time to talk with Granda.

Drew found her grandfather, Howard Davies, at his desk. He listened attentively as Drew went through the harrowing events of her morning. "And Granda, I need to go back and find the cat. The vicar never allowed it outside, and I didn't see it anywhere in the house."

"The constables won't let you back in, Drew Girl." Howard paused momentarily to take off his glasses, then looked up at his granddaughter. "The house will be secured, and everyone will have to stay away, allowing them to do their work. You told them what you found and gave them your name. They know how to reach you should they feel it necessary. You do not need to return to the house."

"Well, I don't need to go inside, as I am sure the cat escaped. I'll go round the back and look in the garden. They didn't really see me when I was there earlier, and I doubt that will change."

"*Nage*, no, not a good idea. Give it a few days. That cat will be just fine. You don't want to be seen anywhere near the scene of the crime. I'll go round to the police station and see if they do need to talk with you again. But in the meantime, no reason for you to return to the vicarage."

Drew, too, supposed the cat would be fine on its own. Maybe even find a mouse to eat. But she was interested in more than the cat. She was the one who found the vicar dead in his bed, and surely that entitled her to information and a look about to see what was taking place. Plus, she really did want to rescue the poor cat. Focusing on that helped keep her mind off what she had seen. Each time the vision of the bloodied corpse played like a cinema reel inside her head, which seemed constant, she would find herself shaking again.

As the end of her day approached, Drew gathered her things to leave. She needed to arrive at the vicarage before dark. Granda was busy on the phone, and she decided not to wait. She was unexplainably drawn back to the vicarage, feeling that the shadows of the dusky day would allow her to enter the grounds unseen. Hopefully the constables would be gone or so busy they wouldn't notice her.

Drew rounded the corner and stopped her bicycle abruptly. She could see people gathered in small groups of twos and threes, quietly talking and looking, some pointing towards the vicarage. The constables were still there, and lights illuminated the inside of the house. The curious on-lookers stood on tiptoe, trying to catch a glimpse through the windows to what was going on inside. By now, the whole village most likely knew of the vicar's death.

Feeling shaken at being at the house once again, Drew took several deep breaths. She pedaled up the lane, then circled round and approached the house from the back. No one was in the back garden. She nonchalantly leaned her bike against the short fence, then leaped over it, landing in the leaves and dead plants of the narrow, unkempt flower beds that lined the backyard. She walked to the back corner of the house, as far from the kitchen window as possible, and was relieved that no constables stood outside and that all the windows and doors were shut. This surprised her, as she thought all the windows and doors would be opened wide to rid the place of the horrible smell of death.

She looked about the grounds as stealthily as possible and then began softly calling the animal. After several long minutes, she heard a low meow. Following the sound and crouching low, she caught a glimpse of orange tucked into a small opening in the foundation. Many of the houses and cottages had root cellars underneath, and she thought this might be what she had found.

Drew got down on her hands and knees and slowly crawled towards the cat's call. All she could see were huge yellow eyes, scared and worried and, she knew, hungry. Lying flat on her stomach, reaching into the dark opening, she pulled the reluctant animal from its hiding place and quickly tucked it tightly into her coat, away from any eyes she might encounter. She made sure there was no one about and once again leaped the fence, boarded her bike with cat in tow and headed home to introduce her furry friend to Nonna.

CHAPTER 3

VESUVI –
THURSDAY, 31 OCTOBER

D rew sat at the kitchen table, stroking the tabby's large head as Nonna watched from her customary place, leaning against the sink with arms crossed in front of her, eyeing the big orange animal.

"You found this brave creature under the vicar's house, you say? How did it come to be outside?"

"The back door to the garden had been jimmied open and left ajar. I assume the cat found its way out the same way the murderer found his way in. Do you think it's a male?"

"How can you not know, Drew? I can see from here he's a brawny boy. Just lift his tail and look at his parts, which certainly match the size of him." Naomi walked to the table and stroked the cat's thick fur. "He's probably several years old. You obviously fed him well."

"He eats more than the vicar, who seldom ate but a few bites of any breakfast or lunch I ever left for the man."

Nonna moved to a shelf and took down a large blue crock filled with risen bread dough. She set it on the table with such a thud the poor creature jumped straight up in the air, landing in front of Drew with a loud *meow*, the large bell round his thick neck rattling with its familiar dull sound.

"That cat erupted like the flames from Vesuvius! Scared the wits out of me," said Nonna, laughing.

Drew picked him up and draped him over her left shoulder, where he snuggled into her neck, his purring loud in her ear. "That is what we will call you, big fellow: Vesuvi. This is your home now." Drew looked to Nonna for agreement, but the older woman merely smiled.

"He's yours to care for, Drew. And best keep him out of Granda's way, as he may not be much for an animal in the house." Nonna paused wistfully before adding, "I do miss having furry companions about, though, and I'm sure Vesuvi will make a nice addition to our home."

Naomi had grown up on a small farm in Italy, surrounded by olive trees, goats, several dogs and any number of cats. She met Howard during the Great War, when he was stationed in Italy, near her town. After the war, before he returned home, he visited her family's farm and proposed marriage to the lovely eighteen-year-old girl with the beautiful brown eyes. She said *si* and left her home and family to join Howard in South Wales, in the beautiful seaside village of Mumbles. They bought a run-down stone cottage on a lovely parcel of land and soon set about restoring it. Together they added another bedroom and bathroom, a shed and a greenhouse, along with a lean-to pen for the chickens and an expansive flower and vegetable garden. The beautifully restored cottage had been Drew's home since she was a very young child.

The telephone rang suddenly, interrupting Drew's thoughts. Nonna walked to the hallway, where the phone sat on a small table in a little niche in the wall. After listening to the caller for a few moments, she said, "*Ie*, yes, Drew found the cat. Does Eira want her brother's cat? Ie, we can keep him. Ie, I will tell her. G'day."

Nonna returned to the kitchen, saying, "That was Mara, calling to let you know the police are finished at the vicar's and asks that you return on Thursday to pack up his papers and personal effects, including his clothes. You're to go by the church at nine a.m., and Mara will have packing boxes waiting for you in the vestibule. She also said you're expected to do a thorough cleaning after the house is emptied and to check on it every week until the new vicar arrives."

Drew nodded, glad to still be earning some additional income. "And what did she ask about a cat, about Vesuvi, I assume?"

"I could hear Eira in the background wanting to know if you knew what happened to Alred's cat. You heard my answer, and when I asked if she wanted it, she said, 'I have no use for cats. Would you be keeping it?' I told her yes."

Drew nodded again. Even though Eira Hughes did not want her brother's cat, at least she had thought to ask if we knew his whereabouts. Drew hugged Vesuvi. "Well, we want you, Great Beastie, and you are home for good."

CHAPTER 4

THE STATION –
FRIDAY, 1 NOVEMBER

A hint of welcome sun greeted Drew as she jumped on her bicycle and pedaled the seven kilometers from Mumbles north to the station in Swansea. It was a beautiful morning, and she never tired of the stunning views of the rugged coastline that accompanied her to work. After the harrowing events of the last week, she looked forward to getting back to her normal schedule.

Drew had worked at the railway station for the past two years. As Granda was Station Master, she had been around trains her entire life, and they had become her passion. Growing up, all she dreamt about was being an engine driver, driving the train from Swansea to London and back again. But the positions of driver, fireman, guard, conductor, porter or other male-dominated positions were not available to women. During the war, because of the scarcity of manpower, women did work in a number of manual jobs as railway employees—the lowest ranking and lowest paying jobs. After the war, the men resumed those positions, as the railway companies and the unions barred women from almost all jobs other than clerical, janitorial, laundry and food service.

Following a year at university in Swansea, where she found the classes boring, the other female students unfriendly, and many of the boys often too friendly, she left school and applied for the open position of Clerical Assistant to the Station Master. Although she was qualified for the position, she knew the primary reason she was given the job was because of Granda. Being the railway station master as well as the dispatcher, all employees at the station were hired and fired by him.

She was initially thrilled to be working for the railway. She knew she did her job well, and she continued to hope there might eventually be an opportunity to rise in the ranks to a position that was currently unattainable. Her goal to drive a locomotive was an aspiration that she had shared only with Sam, and one he told her was impossible since only men could become engine drivers. She still smarted from his comment, but regardless, that was her great ambition and whether unrealistic or not, it didn't change her intention.

As Clerical Assistant to the Station Master, her job included selling tickets, accounting for the monies received and depositing those monies in the bank, making sure each employee turned in their timecards and passing those on to Granda, filing paperwork, managing the assigning of passenger and employee lockers, answering the phones, and whatever other duties she was asked to perform.

She enjoyed working alongside her grandfather every day, but most of all she loved the trains, especially the big steam engines. She loved the way the steam rose high from the tall stacks, the loud hiss of the brakes as the train pulled into the station, the screech of the huge metal wheels on the shiny tracks, the smells of the grease, and watching the churning of those big wheels as they left the station accompanied by the loud whistles.

She never tired of hearing the calls from the guards announcing the trains that were arriving or departing from Swansea, directing the passengers this way or that, and the cacophony of voices coming and going from the carriages as they bid farewell or were greeted by family or friends on the platform. And, if she was honest with herself, most days she also looked forward to seeing Sam.

Drew had an easy manner with the passengers as they stood in the queue each day to buy tickets to wherever they were headed, some friendly and others not so much, but she always offered them courteous help and wished them *"teithiau da,"* good travels, to wherever they were headed. A good majority were men on their way to their offices in London. Some would stay a night or two and then return to their homes in Mumbles or Swansea. Other people might be traveling to London or Cardiff for shopping, or the theatre, or just a day out. Sometimes there were mothers with babies or small children, and Drew loved watching the young ones run amuck in the station, giving the old place some life and much occasion for laughter.

And now, with the end of the fighting in Britain, there were soldiers returning home or passing through to distant parts. Many wore their wounds visibly—bandages, crutches, lost limbs. And others wore their scars inside, wounds of the soul so visible Drew would sometimes catch her breath at the depths of their despair, their auras dark as she looked into their eyes, selling them a ticket to their future.

She walked her bike across the worn hardwood floors of the station towards the glass-fronted offices but slowed her usual quick pace. Through the tall windows, she saw Sam standing beside Granda, looking down at his desk, most likely reviewing the timetables for the day. Quietly entering the room, she slipped her bike into her spot at the back of the office, glad that Sam and Granda were otherwise occupied.

Howard had worked for the railway since the beginning of the First World War. When he enlisted for service, he was assigned to the Railway Operating Battalion. When Drew, ever curious, asked about his experiences during that war, he was always evasive, telling her merely that he was an engine driver and moved troops to and from their destinations. The army is where he learned Morse code, and he could tap out messages in his sleep. She knew he continued to serve in some military capacity during the Second World War, working from the station here in Swansea and often traveling to London to assist with troop movements for the train battalions.

Now that the conflict had ended, Howard spent his days managing employees, coordinating timetables, including delays, changes and any incidents on the platforms, and relaying Morse code messages between stations up and down the lines. Drew admired and respected her granda. As was expected, he ran the railway station with military efficiency and solved problems with seeming ease. He was respectful and fair to all the employees, some having served with him in the war, and in turn, they all respected him. He was especially helpful to the soldiers and nurses returning home and always took time to visit with them. If such could be managed, wounded soldiers were provided a meal from one of the two food vendors in the station as they arrived and departed.

"*Bore da*, good morning, Drew Girl," greeted Granda. "The eight o'clock is thirty minutes late, so be sure to let them know." When the trains were delayed, which was a frequent occurrence, Drew posted a sign in the ticket window along with relaying the information to the passengers buying tickets for the late train. Otherwise, many came back to her window later announcing that she never let them know and a delay was more than inconvenient, voicing their opinion loudly that the railways were poorly run.

"*Diwrnod da*, Drew." Sam's cautious greeting of good day was answered by a curt nod of Drew's head and no eye contact. She noted that he used only her name and didn't call out his usual cheerful greeting of "*Bore da*, Drew Girl!", indicating that he, too, felt lingering remorse from their last conversation. Well, that was not really her concern. She was surprised that she felt remorse at the sting his formal greeting caused.

"I'll open the window early and post the sign," Drew called over her shoulder as she propped her satchel beside her desk. She turned quickly, hurried out the office doors to the lobby and turned to the left, but stopped short of opening the booth.

"*Twimffat!*" Drew said to herself as she realized she forgot her box. Such an idiot! Money for change, tickets, receipts, paper and pens were all sitting in the usual place, locked in the large bottom drawer of her desk. Embarrassed, she reluctantly returned to the office, catching a glimpse of Granda and Sam, both attempting to hide sly smiles from her as she walked haughtily past them to her desk, claimed the ticket box and quickly exited the room.

Her ticket cage, with metal bars spaced half a hand-width apart, most straight up and down in an interesting curve, surrounded her from the waist up to above her head. By the time she opened her window, passengers were queued up twenty or more long. From the office windows, she could feel Sam's eyes frequently glancing her way. She put aside her jumbled feelings and greeted each person with a calm demeanor and welcoming smile as she pointed to the sign hanging in the window announcing the eight o'clock delay. Many bought tickets anyway, hoping the delay would be brief. Some purchased instead a seat on the next train timetabled for London. One train's delay often meant the next scheduled arrival might also be held up. Oh well, this seemed to mirror her life, for she felt delayed as well.

CHAPTER 5

A STRANGER AT THE DOOR –
MONDAY, 4 NOVEMBER

D rew felt an unexpected sense of curiosity, an urgency to get back inside the empty house. She told herself she needed to empty the larder of anything that was spoiled, but in truth, she wanted to walk through the rooms. She assumed the bedroom would be stripped bare, but would she find anything amongst his possessions giving any hint as to what happened in the dark of night in the man's bedroom? And, she was having bad dreams most nights, dreams that mirrored her thoughts and memories during the day. Maybe going back again, seeing the house in daylight, all traces of murder removed before she needed to pack the house up, would put an end to the nightmares.

Approaching the house this Monday, she did not expect to find someone standing on the front stoop. Drew slowed her pedaling and proceeded towards the gate as she took in the figure. Obviously a woman, tall and wearing a dark head scarf tied securely under her chin against the cold wind, a long brown coat, gloves, serviceable brown shoes the same color as her coat, and a handbag in her left hand. Drew concluded she looked a sensible woman.

Walking through the gate, Drew called out to her. "Hello! Can I help you?"

The woman turned, stern-faced, and tugged her handbag up tight to her elbow. "And you are?"

"I'm Drew Davies. I clean—or *had* cleaned the vicar's house several days a week, and I'm here again to set things straight before the new vicar arrives. And you are?"

"Charlotte Parkinson Hughes. I saw the obituary in the paper and came for the funeral."

"Hughes? You knew the vicar?"

Looking away from Drew, the woman raised her chin high and said, "No. He was my father and I did not know him."

"Your father? Vicar Hughes was your father?"

Charlotte shivered and heaved a great sigh, then motioned towards the door. "Can we please go inside before I freeze?"

Curiosity won the day, and Drew unlocked the door and led the way to the kitchen. She laid the long leather strap of her satchel over the arm of one of the chairs and saw the woman look longingly at the one other chair at the table.

"Please sit while I make us tea. I always start my routine here with a cup of tea." In truth, Drew never made tea for herself at the vicarage but knew this woman needed it sooner than later, and what harm would it do? She was, after all, the vicar's daughter.

Charlotte gratefully pulled out the wooden chair and folded herself slowly down onto its hard seat. She just as slowly removed the coat from her shoulders and draped it across the back of the chair, then pulled off her brown leather gloves, one finger at a time, and placed them on top of her handbag sitting on the table. Settled, she immediately turned to her left and gazed silently out the window, as if expecting possibility to walk up the road. Drew filled the kettle and set it on the flame.

Giving Charlotte time and hiding her intense curiosity as best she could, Drew began to rummage quickly through the cupboards looking for tea—the vicar must have had tea—and hopefully a tin of biscuits. Casting glances towards her every few seconds, Drew noticed the woman picking and picking at the cuticles of her nails, a look of anxious dread across her face. The scent of lavender and loneliness emanated from her.

Drew placed the mismatched cups and saucers, napkins and spoons on the table, along with a small bowl of lump sugar and a tin of biscuits of indeterminate age. The kettle whistled, and Drew hurried to douse the flame. "Here we go." Smelling the milk, she found it somewhat acceptable and set the bottle on the table before pouring first for Charlotte and then for herself. "There is still some milk in the bottle, but I cannot attest to how fresh it is." Drew sat in the chair across from the visitor, and together they stared out the window, as the dregs of old leaves left in the bottom of the tin attempted to steep themselves into a semblance of tea.

The minutes passed in silent limbo. Unable to stand the tension, Drew finally said, "I'm not sure if you would welcome condolences at the passing of your father, but I do offer them."

At that, Charlotte turned and looked directly at Drew, her tea still untouched. "Nothing is welcomed nor needed, as nothing is what I feel."

Drew thought this an odd thing to say and obviously wasn't true at all, as everything about the middle-aged woman vibrated emotion and strong feeling. It radiated as a cloudy aura all about her. "Death can arouse many emotions, many of them unexpected and most of them overwhelming." Drew repeated the words sometimes offered to her over the years.

"And how would you, young woman, know anything of death?"

"I lost both my parents suddenly and overnight when I was a very young child. I feel that loss and their absence in my life every day," Drew said softly.

"Well, while I am truly sorry for your loss, mine is different, you see. I never really had a father to mourn. He left my pregnant mother penniless and hopeless before I was born. Her unrelenting grief was the emotional foundation of our lives, and my anger towards her helplessness drove me to flee her—just as he did." Charlotte wondered why she was sharing her pain with this stranger.

"Is your mother still alive, still a part of your life?"

"She passed several years ago. Silent and pitiful to her last day."

"Where did she live? Where do you live?" Drew couldn't help but ask.

"London. I live in London."

They then sipped their warm tea, and Drew ate more stale biscuits than she thought polite, but as usual, she was hungry. The woman didn't eat and did not seem to notice that Drew did.

Drew poured them both more weak tea. "Maybe your father didn't know about you."

"I didn't take you for such a naïve girl. When you leave a woman six months pregnant, obviously you realize the circumstances in which she will soon find herself. And Mother made sure he knew, over and over, over many years until I demanded she stop. Her plaintive humiliation angered me. I just wanted her to get on with whatever life she had left to live. Which she never did."

"And did you get on with your life?" Drew asked quietly.

Charlotte's clothes and her general deportment gave the impression of a woman of some status, of some means. She glanced down and smoothed her wool skirt, saying, "I went to university in London and never left. Literally never left the campus again." She sat taller in her chair and raised her chin. "I became a professor of philosophy and English letters and have lived a mostly dull and uneventful life. But my position afforded me an adequate income for Mother and myself. I was able to purchase a regal old house on the periphery of the campus. Mother attended to the house and gardens, and I attended to my classes and students."

She squared her shoulders, adding, "I eventually made somewhat of a name for myself. Rose up in the querulous ranks of the male-dominated world of academia. By all obvious accounts, yes, I did get on with my life." Charlotte appeared fatigued by her long discourse but also seemed relieved, no longer picking at her fingers.

"I sincerely admire your tenacity. You must be a woman of some courage and persistence. Certainly qualities to admire."

The woman turned stormy eyes on Drew. Eyes filled with regret and grief despite her denials. "I would like to walk through the rooms of this house now, young lady. Alone."

Drew knew the woman was holding her emotions tightly in check and attempting to find surer footing rather than dissolving into a pool of emotions before a stranger. In making the curt request, she was attempting to right herself, and Drew saw no harm in letting her walk through the house.

"The Women's Church Auxiliary tell me the police are done here, so, ie, see yourself around. I'll be here clearing the table. Take as long as you like."

Drew wondered if the vicar left a will, and would this daughter inherit anything he had left behind. Would that even matter to the woman, as perhaps all she had really wanted was a flesh and blood father? At least, that is what Drew assumed she truly wanted, what every child would desire, and that reality was now long lost.

Charlotte walked slowly through the kitchen's curved archway into the front room. Her eyes moved from object to object, taking in the worn sofa with the brightly colored crocheted afghan across its top, the small double-shelved end table beside it with a lamp and telephone, two faded stuffed armchairs on each side of the small fireplace, and the thin drab curtains hanging from the windows. She realized there was no evidence of what life her father lived, other than one of absence—nothing personal or even church-related in sight.

The only other rooms to see were a study, his bedroom, and a bath. Walking first into the bathroom, Charlotte noted the clean, white-tiled floor and white porcelain bathtub, sink and toilet. A small dark wood cabinet with a mirrored front hung above the sink. She didn't hesitate to open the door to see if the contents might reveal something of the man who used this space every day. All to be found were his dentures, a comb, a razor, a ragged toothbrush and coiled tube of toothpaste, one half of a used cake of soap, an almost-empty bottle of cologne that smelled of rotten leaves, and two containers of what appeared to be eye drops. A few bottles of pills for stomach upset, constipation, and a medication from a chemist's shop whose name she did not recognize were lined up on the top shelf. One dingy towel hung from a hook on the back of the door. Otherwise, the room was stark white and devoid of any testimony of the man who looked in this mirror at himself. She thought fleetingly that perhaps his life might not have been so different from her own.

His study was another matter. Papers and books were piled haphazardly across the large oak desk. A stack of files occupied one corner of the desktop beside a large lamp. There was a worn leather chair behind the desk, where he must have sat doing whatever he did day to day as a clergyman, and two smaller chairs on the other side. The only adornment on the walls was a single picture behind his desk. It was dark and religious in nature. Charlotte stepped closer and saw it was a picture of a saint she had never heard of: Saint Charlotte of the Resurrection. Standing stock still, looking intently at the picture of her namesake, Charlotte touched the glass and saw her own reflection as well as the saint's. Suddenly exhausted, she turned to find the accommodating young woman. Today was not the time to go into her father's bedroom.

As she finished drying the last of the dishes, Drew heard Charlotte walking back to the kitchen, her sensible shoes (much the same as Drew's few female professors wore during her short tenure at university) knocking soundly on the wood floor with each step.

"Will you be coming again to clean?" the woman asked.

"Ie, I'm to come every Monday until the new vicar arrives and then probably more often, depending on his preference. Why do you ask?"

"I find myself too tired to look at the stack of papers and files in the study or to look in the bedroom but would like to come back next Monday when you are here again. Is that possible?"

"I don't see why not. I think I am the only one coming round. Do you know if more of your family has been notified? I don't know if the constables took anything away. You know, as evidence."

"Tomorrow I will see those in charge of the investigation and inquire whether my father left a will. I also need to know if there are other children or relatives that I am unaware of.

"I would rather not be here alone. Therefore, I will see you here next Monday, say, seven-thirty again? And what did you say your name was, young lady?"

"Drew Davies. But perhaps I will see you before then. I assume you'll be attending your father's funeral this Saturday?"

"The funeral, of course. Of course I must attend." Charlotte spoke with a note of sarcasm tinged with sadness and began picking once again at the raw skin round her fingernails.

"Perhaps you might meet someone there who could shed some light on any other relatives that might exist. Your father's sister, Eira Hughes, will be there, I'm sure, and she might have some information on the family." Drew watched Charlotte as her gray aura was now outlined with ribbons of red. She felt a rush of sadness and compassion towards this tortured woman. She knew Charlotte was not as tough as she appeared. "And when we meet here again on Monday, Charlotte, I plan to make us a hearty breakfast before we do any more investigating."

Charlotte gathered her belongings from the kitchen table, quickly pulled on her coat, and tied her scarf tight under her chin. She tugged her gloves on fiercely as she walked to the door where she paused, taking stock of the young woman in front of her. She nodded once and said quietly, "Thank you, Drew Davies. You kept my father's house very clean."

CHAPTER 6

THE CURIOUS MAN – WEDNESDAY, 7 NOVEMBER

Drew saw him standing there in the queue, third down the line behind the woman in front of her ticket window. She realized he was the same well-put-together gentleman who traveled back and forth from London every other Thursday morning, London to Swansea, then Swansea to London on the same day.

"Are you the girl that cleans the vicar's house?" he asked when he stood in front of her. Not "Ticket to London please." or "Is the train on time today?".

"Are you buying a ticket?"

"I understand that you cleaned his house and fed his cat. You must have seen the cat every day. Have you seen the cat lately?"

"No, I did not see a cat the last time I was there."

"And when was the last time you were there?"

"Why are you asking me these questions? Are you buying a ticket or not? If not, please step aside so I can sell tickets to those who are."

The man in the bowler hat gave Drew a taut look of frustration and stepped away from her iron-grilled window. She watched him walk towards the main door, then pause and stand a few moments, looking back at her as though collecting his thoughts before leaving.

Drew quickly sold the remaining passengers their tickets, not engaging them in general chitchat as she usually would. When the train was announced and the passengers headed to the platform exit behind her, Drew closed her window and quickly walked to the front entrance, hoping to catch sight of the man looking for a cat. The vicar's cat, now Drew's cat.

She caught a glimpse of his black bowler as he rounded the corner before crossing the street. He turned once on the other side and looked back towards the station. Drew quickly pressed against the station's stone wall, hoping he hadn't seen her. Why is this man looking for Vesuvi? She didn't recall ever seeing the vicar and this man together at the station, but obviously he knew the vicar, knew he had a cat. But what could he want with Vesuvi? She needed to find out who this man in the bowler hat was and why all the questions.

Back inside the station, she saw there were no new passengers in the queue. She hurried to the office, finding Granda sitting at his desk sending a teletype. She sat down at her own desk and fiddled with papers, trying to wait patiently for her grandfather to finish.

Howard completed the message and sat back in his chair. "I see you are ready to burst, Drew Girl. What is it?"

"Is there a way to find out the identity of a passenger?"

"And why would you be asking?"

"There is a man, a large man who always wears a bowler hat and a long dark wool coat. He carries a briefcase and travels every other Thursday from London to Swansea and back again the same day. Just now, he was in my queue and asked me if I was the girl who cleaned the vicar's house and where was the vicar's cat."

"And what did you tell him?"

"I told him I hadn't seen the cat at the vicarage since the man died. Which is true. I asked him why he was questioning me. He quickly left the queue and walked out of the station. I watched him cross the street and disappear behind a building. Can we find out who he is?"

"I suppose we can, but not in any official way, since no one is required to show identification when buying a ticket, and we can't ask that they do so. Since he travels back and forth twice a month, I would assume someone must know the gent."

"We know the vicar did, and as the police are conducting a murder investigation, I would think they would want to know this man is asking questions. I think I'll go see whoever is in charge and let them know."

"Let me put in a call to Lewis and see what he says. In the meantime, Drew, you leave it for now. He might have merely been a friend of the vicar's and is just asking after his cat."

"I very much doubt that to be the case. He was rude and demanding. But as long as the man leaves me alone, I will do the same. He certainly isn't coming anywhere near Vesuvi."

Drew listened as her granda rang the police station and asked for Chief Inspector Lewis. They exchanged cordial greetings, each asking after the other's family, and Drew realized they were quite familiar with each other. After describing the man and relaying the questions "one of my railway employees asked," it was obvious the officer had no further questions, and Granda ended the call.

"Lewis said he would look into it but didn't seem very interested. Perhaps they have a sound lead as to who the murderer is and are close to wrapping it up."

"But it's still odd that the man wanted to know about Vesuvi," Drew persisted, as she headed out once more to the ticket window. She turned and added, "He did not strike me as someone who would care about the fate of a lost cat."

CHAPTER 7

THE WOMEN'S CHURCH AUXILIARY – THURSDAY, 7 NOVEMBER

Borrowing Granda's small lorry for the morning, Drew drove to the church. The bed of the vehicle would have plenty of room for the vicar's belongings. She found Mara Roberts waiting for her inside the vestibule, where six large boxes sat at her feet. Always smartly appointed, today Mara's well-coiffed gray hair was pulled in a tight bun at the base of her neck, setting off the subtle gold of her small, round earrings. Her dark blue skirt and tailored blouse matched the blue of her eyes. She held her gloves in one hand, gently slapping them into the palm of the other, radiating an intense energy. Her three-quarter-sleeve black jacket with an animal's tail hanging from the collar lay across one of the boxes, her hat resting on top.

"Here you are, Miss Davies. We want everything out before the interim vicar arrives—which should be within the next two weeks or so, although they keep moving the date, which is exceedingly frustrating.

"So you know, Miss Davies, I checked with the authorities, and they have gone through the vicarage top to bottom, examining all the vicar's belongings and papers. Anything they thought might be helpful in the investigation they already took with them. I told them if they need any of what remains, we will be storing boxes here at the church. Eira will, of course, go through it as she is able . . . sometime after the funeral, as she is in no state to do so now."

Eira Hughes, the vicar's sister, was someone Drew was sure she had met sometime over the years but today could not place her face. And this woman would be Charlotte's aunt. Had either known of the other's existence? "Has there been any news from the constables regarding who might have broken in and killed the vicar? Any suspects or leads?"

"Suspects or leads? Dear heavens no, not that I have heard, and nothing has been reported in the papers. Why do you ask? Have you heard something I have not?"

"No, no. I am sure you, being on the church council, would have heard before me, and I have not heard anything. And I agree, there's been nothing in the papers. Just curious as to why there hasn't been some sort of update or statement."

"You're correct in that. If there was anything to report, I'm sure I would have heard almost immediately and then it would most assuredly have been in the paper," said Mara, rapping her gloves soundly against her palm.

Returning once more to the task assigned her, Drew said, "I assume you want all the furniture and kitchen items left as is, and you're only talking about my packing up personal items—the books and papers from the study, what is in the bathroom, and his clothes?"

"Yes, all of that. Just pack all that up," she said, hands fluttering like birds, "and Eira can worry about it later. Eira and Alred were not on the best of terms these last couple of years, and she tells me she is not interested in whatever he left behind. And remember, we want you to do a thorough cleaning before the new man comes in. And drop in every Monday to check that there is nothing amiss and give a quick dusting. You'll be paid accordingly."

Drew knew the woman was in a rush to have her take the boxes and leave so she could get on about her day. But she also knew this moment in time was the only opportunity she might have to get information. "Did you know the

Vicar Hughes well, Mrs. Roberts?" she asked, picking up two of the empty boxes.

"I suppose so. Well enough to know he was a sad, lonely man. How strange that someone would kill such a solitary person, much less a man of the clergy."

"Why do you say he was sad and lonely?"

"From the Great War, you know. He never wanted to talk about it, but you could see tragedy written all over him. And the way his eyes constantly watered . . . from the gassings, I suspect. We all felt that his pain from those years drove him to seek refuge in the ministry. But it was obvious the life of a clergyman never really suited him. He preferred to isolate himself rather than tend to his congregation. Ie, we all saw the pain."

"Who is the 'we' you refer to, Mrs. Roberts?"

"We of the Women's Church Auxiliary, of course. Those who probably knew him best. And then his dear sister, Eira. She is actually the one that put his name forward when a vacancy occurred here in 1925. From the day he arrived, we ladies felt we ministered to him rather than the other way round. That never changed in twenty years. In retrospect, of course, it was not a good decision, his coming here to our parish. Eira soon saw that as well, but the die was cast and so there we were. Oh well, women do what they need to do to keep all things moving forward, often in less than desirable circumstances.

"You get to know a person, even one as withdrawn as Alred Hughes, when you take them dinner once a week, which we all took turns doing over the many years. And not just the war widows, but the married ones too. We all understood hardship and loneliness, and you only had to look at those sad eyes to see he must have suffered greatly. We always wondered what atrocities of war he endured and who might have been lost to him. Many of us didn't really believe those watery eyes were just from the gas."

"Did anyone come to know anything more about his past before the war, before he came to Swansea?"

"I never heard about any of that, and of course, I would have been told had he shared anything like that with the auxiliary ladies. Eira said he was as closed to her as he was with everyone. I know she visited with him frequently at the vicarage, and even though she and I are good friends, she never mentioned their conversations. When I once asked, she avoided the topic, saying it wasn't anyone's concern. Over the last several years, she has become almost as distant as her brother. We are not as close as we once were."

Mara sighed and continued, "Regarding where he came from before taking the post here, his papers from the Anglican Church office said he had requested a transfer, but they didn't indicate from where and neither the vicar nor Eira, if she knew, ever said. That was always a puzzle. You have to wonder why all the secrecy."

"Thank you for taking the time to chat, Mrs. Roberts. I'll just get these boxes into the car and begin packing up and thoroughly cleaning the vicarage this week. And as you instructed, I will look in on the house on Mondays. Oh, and do you know if the church will be keeping me on to cook and clean for the new vicar?"

"I think that is a question we will have to ask the new man when he gets here. And if so, which I would think highly probable, then we will let you know, Miss Davies. We believe you did a suitable job of it with Alred, and that has been appreciated." Mara handed Drew an envelope she knew to be her wages, and the older woman took her leave.

Making two trips to Granda's lorry, Drew stowed the boxes in the back, stuffed the money envelope into the depths of her satchel and drove away from the church with more questions than answers.

CHAPTER 8

PASTA WITH NONNA – FRIDAY, 8 NOVEMBER

At four p.m., Drew jumped aboard her bike and headed home to Mumbles. She rode quickly past the long pier looking out towards Lighthouse Island. The days were getting shorter, colder as well, and she was eager to get home to make Friday pasta with Nonna. She looked forward to this weekly ritual, the warm kitchen and Nonna's even warmer presence. It was a special time together, and Drew never tired of the shared experience where she always seemed to learn something new about cooking, about Nonna, and, most of all, about herself.

She heard the music before she reached the cottage and stopped her bike to listen as she watched the last of the day's light reflected on the gray and tan flagstones of their lovely home. She wondered if her father, whose bike she now rode, had ever stopped here and admired his house in the last light of such a day.

Smoke rose high from the chimney above the kitchen, casting long fingers of gray into the sky, beckoning Drew in. She had shared the home with her father's parents since the age of four, when her mother, father, and older brother, Matteo, died. The night she was told they would not be coming home was Drew's earliest memory in the twenty years of her life. A life forever changed by the telling. She was acutely aware that there was always something unsettled in her, a desperation to find answers to what happened to her family. But today, on this Friday, she was eager to join the warmth that awaited her and let go of the pervasive sullenness and her feelings of frustration.

Earlier at the station, Granda had commented on her melancholy, reminding her that it really had nothing to do with Sam. It was the time of year, the season when her parents had left her, left all of them. And with the vicar's murder, she wondered again if her family's deaths could have been more than a tragic accident and who could have been responsible.

These were familiar questions and ones that had tumbled round and round her mind for years: Were there individuals who knew more about the death of her family? Why had they died? She never believed it was an accident. Shaking such maudlin thoughts from her head, she rode on to her home and the welcome relief it would bring.

"What pasta are we making today?" Drew asked loudly over the strains of *Aida*, her grandmother's operatic choice for this week.

"In honor of your furry friend, so calm until he erupts, today we make pasta Vesuvio."

"There is a pasta named after a volcano—and my cat? That is really quite remarkable."

"Our Vesuvio pasta may not look exactly like those made by the famous pasta makers of Gragnano, in Naples, but we will do our best!"

Nonna was a connoisseur of opera and a master pasta maker. Before the war, when there were enough people requesting, she would teach a Saturday class advertised as "How to Make Authentic Italian Pasta." Depending on where the requests came from, the class was held either in Mumbles or Swansea, and Italian opera music always played softly in the background.

After years of watching and practicing the art of pasta making and still considering herself a novice, Drew knew what those in the class did not: creating authentic Italian, hand-rolled pasta was indeed an art. An art that took years to perfect.

She mentioned this to Nonna when she first began teaching the classes, and her grandmother responded, "Si, that is true, Drew, but every artist must start at the beginning. Making fine pasta is a journey, and I am merely the muse sparking their interest. Many, though they may enjoy the class, will lose interest shortly after, most will never become proficient, and the few that persist will realize it is an art form that requires skill and brings great satisfaction, both to the stomach and to the soul. And that is the great joy of art. You do not need to become a Michelangelo to appreciate the beauty and magic of the experience."

Throughout the conversation, Vesuvi sat on Drew's lap, watching Nonna scoop flour onto her treasured pasta board. Wooden squares laid in opposite directions created a textured surface that produced what Nonna called a "cat's tongue" texture, important in rolling out the pasta. Nonna was proud that both her family's cherished pasta board and *mattarello*, the long thin rolling pin, were given to her when she left Naples and journeyed to Wales. The old board and rolling pin, along with a pasta cutter used by generations of women in her family, were the greatest gifts her mother could have given her, a sacrifice and an offering wishing Naomi well in her new country and a reminder to never forget the one she was leaving behind.

"You are quiet, Drew. What are your thoughts today, my girl?"

"I keep thinking about the murder and also about Charlotte, the vicar's daughter, and how terrible it would be not to have a family. I told you we had tea at the vicarage and how she was so desolate and wore her grief wrapped round her like her heavy wool coat. I saw terrible sorrow in her aura; dark shadows played all round her. The force of it was so strong it almost frightened me. I am so grateful and thankful for you and Granda, but Charlotte's loss made me feel my own grief all the more." Drew hugged her great orange cat before finally looking up into Nonna's eyes.

Nonna broke three fresh eggs, from their generous hens, into the center of the semolina flour and began blending the bright yellow yolks and the iridescent whites together. She then pulled small amounts of flour from all sides into the center, mixing the eggs with the fine white flour until a firm ball of dough was formed. With strong hands, she kneaded the dough on the board's surface for six minutes, then covered it with a thin tea towel to rest for thirty minutes more.

The resting would allow the gluten strands to soften, and the dough would be ready for rolling.

Nonna wiped her hands on her apron and sat down beside her beloved granddaughter. As always, she saw her own sorrow mirrored in Drew's eyes. "It is a terrible thing not to know your parents, and her grief, as you tell me, is made even more painful knowing she was rejected by her father. You know, Drew, your own parents loved you completely from the moment you were born. Nothing but tragedy would have separated them from you. You know that in your soul, do you not, my girl?"

"Ie, I do. I always feel their love, their presence. But that doesn't make my missing them any less. We *were* separated. They're gone forever and I am still here, and I still don't know the full story of what happened to them. I know you understand, Nonna. They were yours too. You must feel the same pain.

"I know we don't talk about it often, but the sadness is a part of all our lives. Why won't you and Granda tell me if there is more to their story? I feel you both know more than you say. I am a grown woman, Nonna. They were my family too, and I deserve to know the truth. I cannot live the rest of my life not knowing."

"I don't know more than what you have already been told. Your parents and Matteo had been in London visiting friends. You stayed with us because you had a fever. On the way home, there was an accident. The car careened off the road, dropped down a steep cliff, caught fire, and they were gone."

"But why did the car go off the road? Was it raining? Foggy? Icy? Was the car hit from behind or in front by another car, pushing it over the side? And if so, what happened to that other car? Would they just drive away? And if so, again, why?"

"It wasn't stormy that autumn night. The weather was mild and dry. We just do not know how they came to fall over the side. The car was damaged going down the cliff and was completely destroyed in the fire, so there was no way to determine if it had been struck by another vehicle. I have no answers to your other questions, dearest girl."

"Do you think the police thoroughly investigated? I keep thinking Granda knows more."

"You can ask him. I have many times, and many times he has told me to let it be. He feels that nothing but pain can come of asking questions with no answers."

Drew laid her head against her nonna's shoulder and closed her eyes against the tears threatening to slip down her young face.

Naomi gathered Drew into her arms. "We are thankful every day that you stayed with us that night, or we would have lost our entire world. I know that doesn't make our grief any more bearable or our missing them any more tolerable. But we are blessed that you were spared, and we, the three of us, have made a family."

As much as Drew was comforted by Nonna's words, she still wanted answers. Her father would not have lost control of their car, not on a dry familiar road he had driven all his life. And Granda's reticence to talk about that night, to at least be willing to discuss what might have happened, reinforced her belief that he was withholding what he thought she might find painful. But Drew felt the greatest pain came from not knowing, and answers would provide some closure.

She knew her nature was to question, to want to know details, find answers, and to not settle for simple explanations. Her curiosity, her need to understand or question the status quo often resulted in her finding herself in situations that were sometimes uncomfortable, especially for others when she bombarded them with questions. Her professors had often told her she asked too many questions. One reason she left school was because most so-called answers were often less than satisfactory and even illogical.

Drew often tried to let go of what she realized was petty or didn't make a difference in the end, such as why so much work at the railway seemed duplicated when changes she wanted to suggest would improve efficiency. And, more importantly, why women were still barred from professions traditionally held only by men. During the war, women had worked in the factories, plowed the fields, run companies, and tended to all things that had been done by the men. But now that the war had ended, the answer to why the changes could not be made was usually "because that is the way it has always been done." Meaning the way *men* had always done things. But it was almost 1947, time for change and time for women to assume a larger role in the decisions made in the world. Drew was determined to be part of that change.

Naomi and Drew sat for several minutes, each thinking her own thoughts. Finally, Nonna took Drew's head in her hands, kissed her on the forehead and rose from her chair. She turned the record over and tested her dough. "Come roll the dough, my girl. Put all your feelings into rolling the dough, it has always worked for me. And we will make the Vesuvi. Come now, come help your nonna."

Drew set Vesuvi on the floor, washed her hands, and reached for the apron Nonna held out to her. When the dough was ready to be rolled, you had to set aside any other thoughts. It was a relief to do so.

Drew rolled and rolled until the dough was so thin she could see her fingers through it. Then Nonna picked up her treasured pasta knife, cut into the dough and quickly created dozens of small spiral-shaped volcanos. The two women laughed as Drew attempted time and again to cut and shape the pasta as her grandmother did. Finally, the older woman gently guided the younger's hands, and together they created art.

A day of troubled thoughts was ending. Knowing she would have a delicious dinner with her family, Drew felt, in that moment, contentment.

CHAPTER 9

COFFEE WITH GRANDA –
SATURDAY, 9 NOVEMBER

Vesuvi jumped on Drew's head at precisely six a.m. How could anything, human or beast, be hungry at six a.m.? Sometimes Drew could sleep a little longer if Vesuvi could be coaxed underneath her thick quilts. This morning, however, the cat proved more persistent than usual and refused to snuggle back down to sleep.

"Alright, you demanding beastie! Hush yourself and give me a minute."

Drew reluctantly shed the layers of her warm coverings and reached for her well-worn dressing gown at the end of the bed. She pulled it on while wriggling her feet into her slippers and walked with half-open eyes into the kitchen.

Granda was already up drinking his coffee and reading the three newspapers he and Drew shared weekly. Now why couldn't the cat have just asked him for breakfast? But Drew knew that the cat, if he wanted to remain a resident of the cottage, was wise enough to know who to ask and who to leave be.

"Morning, Drew Girl. You're up awfully early. Vesuvi had his way again? Like some coffee?"

"Let me get Vesuvi his breakfast and then I would love some coffee."

Drew filled the cat's bowl part way with chicken scraps, put fresh water in the other bowl and placed them both on a small tea towel just outside her room.

"Thank you, Granda," said Drew, sitting down across from him, a steaming cup of coffee waiting for her. He always drank his black, but knowing Drew preferred hers with milk, he had added a splash to her cup.

"The vicar's funeral notice is in the paper again. Today at eleven. Will you be joining Nonna and me for this event? I can only imagine the gossip, tinged with intrigue, as every attendee glances round trying to see if the murderer attends," Howard said, raising his eyebrows and smiling. "They say killers do that, you know."

"And you find yourself amusing this morning, Granda? Of course I will be going. I already told Charlotte I would see her there."

"And you've spoken to your new friend much since your tea at the vicar's house?" said Howard playfully as he turned another page.

"You're certainly full of quips and wry comments this morning. What did you put in this coffee? It makes me afraid to drink mine."

"I know you, Drew Davies. Your ears will be tuned to the highest frequencies at this funeral, the better to hear the speculations and rumors you hope will provide some bit of information. Isn't that what the crime solvers in your mystery novels do?"

"Ie, they do, and I will today as well! What better place to listen to rumors that may hold a nugget of truth and look for viable suspects than at the victim's funeral? Although murders in novels seem all full of intrigue and suspense, today feels more about sadness and regret."

"As true as that is, if the culprit is one of our own, he could indeed be hiding in plain sight. Or maybe someone was hired to do the job and then vanished," surmised Howard, eyes still on the newsprint.

"Either is possible," agreed Drew. "I'm suspicious of the man in the bowler hat. No one seems to know anything about him, including your friend in the police, other than he was a frequent passenger on the train to and from London. I have sold him dozens of round-trip tickets over the past year. I would think the authorities would have questioned him thoroughly.

"And Charlotte, although I feel badly for her, I sense she is hiding something. She doesn't seem the violent type, but murderers come in all shapes and sizes."

"And you deduced that truth from your latest Agatha Christie novel?" teased Granda.

"You know that to be true, and all the more reason I would think the authorities would be at the funeral checking out suspects. At any rate, I will, as you say, keep my curious eyes and ears open." Drew rose and gave Granda a kiss on his cheek before pouring herself more coffee and adding another dash of milk.

"Regardless," Howard began seriously, "it will be a coming together of familiar people and community, and that is something we haven't done much of these past years. Even under the circumstances, I think it will be good for us. I wonder what the auspicious ladies of the auxiliary will serve at the reception. I dropped some eggs and a bag of potatoes off at Mara's yesterday, thinking they could make use of them. She said they planned to make casseroles, so hopefully that will help feed the multitudes with whatever they all have to spare."

"That was kind of you, Granda. You are always kind. A rapscallion, but a kind one." Drew smiled lovingly at her grandfather and downed the last of her coffee as he returned a wry smile and a military salute.

She was planning on returning to bed for another hour or so of sleep but on second thought sat back down and quietly asked, "Were there many people at Mother, Father and Matteo's funeral?"

Her grandfather was still for a long moment before slowly folding his newspaper and laying it on the table. "Ie, girl. There were many people who attended, and many of those same people will be at this funeral today."

"You didn't take me with you to the funeral, so who did I stay with?"

"Serena came here and stayed with you till we returned home."

They sat in silence for some minutes. "I worry that I will forget them, Granda. I was so young and have only the faintest of memories."

"You know they will always be with us, Drew Girl."

"We can say that, but it doesn't make me miss them less. I feel the loss every day. It is like a sad hole in my heart."

Howard reached across the table and took Drew's hands in his own. "Ie, there will always be that hole. Nonna and I feel it, of course we do. We try every day to fill it with our love for you."

Suddenly overcome with fatigue, Drew rose from her chair, wiping her eyes, and gave Granda a tight hug. She rinsed her cup and returned to her room where she found Vesuvi asleep and purring loudly on her pillow. She gently scooted him over and settled her head down beside his as she drifted back to sleep. She was not looking forward to the funeral. Dreaded the thought of it, actually. This was the first one she would have attended. Hopefully, the next few hours of sleep would help numb her misgivings.

CHAPTER 10

THE FUNERAL –
SATURDAY, 9 NOVEMBER

When Drew and her family entered the church, those having already arrived were in loose arrangements sitting in pews towards the front of the church. Most in attendance were at least as old as her grandparents, and she wondered if anyone her age had even known the vicar.

Drew reluctantly followed her grandparents down the aisle, moving slowly forward towards the closed casket where Eira Hughes and a middle-aged man stood with a clergyman.

"That's Eira's son, Jac," Nonna whispered as they got closer.

Drew wondered where the clergyman had traveled from and if he was to be the interim vicar. In appearance, he was almost an exact replica of Alred Hughes. Were Anglican vicars all rather old and sad looking? She hoped the next vicar would have something to offer his congregation other than despair.

As they stood in front of Eira and Jac, Granda and Nonna expressed quiet condolences and stood aside for Drew to do the same. No words came to her, as her eyes were fastened onto the large shiny mahogany casket, closed and sealed for all eternity. All she could muster was a tearful nod before turning round and following her grandparents to a row of pews halfway down the right side. Drew sat between them and quickly wiped her eyes when Nonna offered both a handkerchief and a gentle hand to her arm. She nodded again, this time to reassure Nonna that she was fine, which she was not. Sorrow and grief rolled over her with each ragged breath. This was the funeral she never attended.

The clergyman must have made some sign indicating the service was to begin. People quietly finished filling the pews, and Drew watched Charlotte take a seat directly in front of her. Neither acknowledged the other, but Drew was very sure they were both aware and somehow glad they at least knew one other person. She would speak to Charlotte after the service and introduce her to Granda and Nonna.

Drew thought the short service was barren and lifeless. She felt heavy spirits swirling in the cold air moving about the church and shivered. Was Alred's spirit among them? Other than a brief eulogy and a dark scripture reading by Eira from the book of Job, there was no reminiscing or sharing of peoples' experiences with the vicar. Maybe that would happen after, at the reception. Or could this man have had so little effect on the lives of these people he had served for twenty years that there was nothing much to say? She wondered what was read at her parents' and brother's service and if anyone had spoken about their lives. Did they offer any stories or praise as to the fine people they had been? More questions for Granda.

The room breathed a collective sigh of relief as the clergyman invited everyone into the common room for refreshments, provided by the good ladies of the Women's Church Auxiliary, and for "a time of remembering." Drew hoped the time was infused with a least a little life after such a strangely somber service. But what did she know, this being her first funeral and, she hoped, the last for many years?

Drew and her grandparents waited until most everyone had left their pews before joining the others. As he was about to leave the church, Drew spotted the constable that she had briefly spoken to at the vicarage the day she found the body. She hurried down the aisle and caught him at the bottom of the church steps.

"Excuse me, Constable. Could I please speak with you for a few moments?"

He turned, reluctant and bored. "I need to be on my way. What is it you want?"

"You might remember me. I am the one that found Vicar Hughes . . . dead in his bedroom. We spoke when I was at the station the following day giving my statement."

"No, I don't remember you." With that he turned and began walking away.

Drew followed him. "Just a couple questions. Please, Constable."

Never turning back round, but continuing to walk away, he said, "This murder has nothing to do with you, girly, so go back to selling your railway tickets and leave the rest to the authorities."

Frustrated but knowing futility when she saw it, Drew stopped and watched the man's stout figure receding. She returned to the church and found her grandparents. Charlotte was there, standing off to the side alone, observing the people who actually knew her father. Drew led Granda and Nonna across the room to the vicar's daughter.

"Hello, Charlotte. It's good to see you again. I want you to meet my grandparents, Howard and Naomi Davies."

"Thank you for coming over to say hello, Drew. I know no one here, which is, of course, the way it is." She turned to Howard and Naomi and said, "I must tell you, I have very much enjoyed the help and company of your Drew. You have a fine granddaughter."

"Thank you for your kind words. We certainly think so," said Granda, extending his hand to Charlotte and smiling. "She has shared with us your unfortunate situation, and may we offer our sincere condolences. Will you be returning to London soon or staying on, perhaps waiting for some news of the circumstances of your father's death?"

With a slight sad smile, Charlotte nodded her head, then stood a little taller with her chin raised in resolution, a posture now familiar to Drew. "I have decided to remain in Mumbles for a bit. I am on sabbatical and have some weeks remaining and truly have nothing that awaits me in London until the next term at university begins. And, yes, I do hope there is news regarding my father's demise before I leave. Your town is charming, and I find being by the water is both soothing and expansive to the spirit. You are fortunate to live in such a beautiful place."

"Perhaps while you're here you might join us one evening for dinner. We would enjoy hearing about your academic life at university. I wish we also had something to share regarding your father, but we did not belong to his congregation and did not know him, really, at all," said Nonna.

"By the tone of the service and lack of speakers, it seems as though no one knew him well. I know his sister Eira is here, but we have not met."

Drew put her hand on Charlotte's arm. "Would you like me to introduce you? She was the woman who gave the scripture reading. Perhaps you and she might set up a time to visit."

"Yes, I would very much like that," said Charlette, looking hopefully about the room for who might be her aunt.

Drew scanned the room, finding Eira beside the buffet table, chatting with other women from the church. Taking Charlotte's arm, she led her towards the vicar's sister.

"Excuse me, Miss Hughes. I want to introduce you to Charlotte Parkinson Hughes. You and she have some common connection to your brother."

"Connection to Alred? And what might that be?" Eira sounded more angry than curious as she looked stiffly at Charlotte.

"Hello, Eira. While this may come as a surprise, or maybe you knew, I am your brother's daughter. He left my mother before I was born. Neither my mother nor I ever saw or heard from him again, but I am most happy to meet you and am so sorry for your loss."

Grabbing hold of the table, Eira said in a hoarse voice just above a whisper, "Of course you never heard from him. You are a fraud. My brother had no family other than myself and my son, Jac. My brother never married, and he had no children, certainly none that can claim rightful paternity." Eira's countenance turned vicious as her voice rose to a pitch and volume all could hear. "How dare you impose yourself here today! What a thoughtless and vile thing to do. You are not welcome here and you need to leave—now!"

Jac moved quickly between his mother and Charlotte. "You have no business here. You have nothin' to do with our family."

Charlotte stood rooted in place. "Please think it over, Eira. I am not your enemy," she said quietly. "I want nothing from you other than to learn about my father. Like it or not, we *are* family and could perhaps get along. I will be staying in Mumbles for some weeks, should you change your mind."

With all eyes watching, Charlotte turned and regally walked across the common room and out the door to the lawn. Drew began to follow her but Granda, who had come over to intervene if necessary, caught her hand.

"Let her go. She'll be fine. I have no doubt she is as strong a woman as she appears."

Granda added that after they left the church he was stopping by the station, and on his way would drop Nonna at Serena's for a visit and would pick her up on his way back. Drew needed fresh air and time by the water and said she would appreciate the walk home. They all agreed to be back at the cottage by dinner.

Drew stayed only a short while longer, taking a moment to look about the room, hoping to capture a sense of what people were feeling before making her own exit. She hoped Charlotte might still be somewhere about the church grounds, but she was nowhere in sight. To be honest, Drew was glad to be alone.

The air was sharp in the pale late-afternoon light. Deep breaths filled Drew's fatigued spirit, bringing some renewal. Her thoughts were spinning in her mind as she headed towards the bay. She made her way down the embankment to the shore and walked along the water's edge, contemplating the latest events. Did Eira know of Charlotte's existence before today? Her inflamed response to Charlotte would suggest she did know her brother had a child. She did not seem particularly shocked or surprised but most extraordinarily angry. Quite an odd reaction, really. Perhaps Eira found it embarrassing that Charlotte would have the gall to attend her brother's funeral.

The sharp calls of seabirds filled the air as they swirled and flew in arcs high above the water as Drew climbed up towards the road and started for home. Looking back at the birds in restless flight, Drew thought they looked exactly like her thoughts.

As she walked on, she thought more about the funeral and many questions and observations rose to her mind. People who appeared to be the only relatives of the vicar displayed little to no sorrow. Eira was more emotional at meeting Charlotte than she was over the loss of her brother. And Charlotte? She seemed merely disappointed by the shunning of her only relatives. And from what Charlotte had shared with Drew, she obviously blamed her father for her mother's lifelong despair and, most likely, her own empty life as well. The question Drew found herself pondering was whether either woman, Charlotte or Eira, bore Alred Hughes enough ill will to commit murder.

She was nearly home by the time the sun was just touching the horizon and the cold was touching her bones. Approaching the cottage, she saw no smoke rising from the chimney, meaning she was the first to arrive and would immediately set a fire in the kitchen grate and begin dinner.

She stepped up to the door and stopped dead still. The door was ajar, the lock tampered with and the wood round the knob splintered. She spun around, looking to see if anyone was about, on the street or in the neighbor's garden, but of course, there was no one. She cautiously pushed the door open, peering into the dark kitchen. Was someone still in their home? She did not sense a presence and felt an anger rising that would more than protect her from anyone inside.

She opened the door wider and stepped into the kitchen. It was in complete disarray. Items on the shelves had been thrown to the floor, pottery and glass lay broken in sharp shards. Cupboards and drawers were open and empty, all contents flung across the room. Picking her way carefully to the other side of the kitchen, she looked into the sitting room. There, too, she saw nothing but disorder. Furniture and lamps were turned on end. Magazines and papers were torn and tossed round the room, and Nonna's porcelain figurines lay scattered on the rug, some broken.

She made her way to her grandparents' room. The intruder, or intruders, had been there too. Drew could barely contain her anger at whoever had violated their home in such a vicious manner.

Thinking suddenly of Vesuvi, she rushed to her own room. Where was her cat? She began calling his name over and over as she looked about her room that lay in shambles. Her mattress was askew on the bed, sliced open in deep ragged cuts with the insides pulled out and thrown about. Shelves were overturned, her beloved collection of books scattered haphazardly across the floor, the drawers and wardrobe nearly empty, all her clothes and belongings trampled upon. And no Vesuvi.

Furious and worried, she ran back outside. "Vesuvi! Vesuvi!" She looked all about the property for him. He was nowhere. She neither heard him nor felt his presence nearby. Who would do this! And why?

She needed to clean up the terrible destruction in the kitchen before Granda and Nonna returned. Nonna would be so distraught and Granda—she could not imagine his reaction.

Taking the broom and the mop bucket, she swept the debris into piles, salvaging whatever she could, which was almost nothing, and laying it on the kitchen table. All else she scooped into the bucket, making three trips to the dust bin before loading a stack of wood into her arms. She felt warm tears running down her face as she walked again through the damaged door and attempted to lay a fire in the hearth. The heat of the flames was soothing as she mopped the floor and wiped down the counters and shelves, trying desperately to erase any vile mark of the perpetrator, the one bringing destruction to their good home.

Finally, the kitchen was cleared. So much was lost. What was undamaged or broken but still usable she placed on the table. It was a meager collection of chipped plates, cups without handles, a few platters and bowls, scarred but serviceable, and their eating utensils. She then managed to put the sitting room into some semblance of order just as Granda and Nonna walked in.

"Drew, where are you! Are you alright? What's happened?" asked a shocked Nonna, looking round the battered kitchen.

Broom in hand, Drew looked forlornly at her grandparents. "I don't know how much is missing, but so much has been broken it is hard to tell. Thank goodness your pasta board and mattarello were left alone." The relief of having her grandparents in the house brought tears flooding from her eyes.

Howard stepped forward and wrapped Drew in a strong hug. She felt safe in his arms. Then she took a deep breath and began wiping her tears away. He stepped back, put his hands on her shoulders and looked directly into her eyes.

"You are alright, Drew. That is what is important. Tell me, did you see anyone leaving or about the property as you approached the house, or see anyone suspicious you may have crossed paths with as you walked home?"

"No. I didn't see anyone, but it was almost dark. I think the person who did this left sometime before I got here. The house was as cold as ice when I walked in, so the door must have been open for some time. And Vesuvi is gone. I can't find him anywhere."

"You know how cats are, Drew Girl. They are wily, cunning beasts, and I am sure he took off and hid when the ruckus started. He has been through this before. He'll keep watch, and when all is quiet, he'll venture back home."

It was Nonna's turn to engulf her in comforting arms. "Oh, my Drew, sit with us and tell us what you found when you walked through the door. I cannot believe this has happened."

And Drew did, step by step. She told them what she found from the moment she saw the door ajar and that the lock had been jimmied. That she did not want them to come home and find their kitchen completely torn asunder and that she had tried to tidy it all, saving what she could.

Howard listened intently as he stood silently in the middle of the kitchen, looking slowly in all directions. He then began to circle the room, examining every surface, cupboard and shelf. Going into the other rooms, he did the same—stood in the center, taking in everything and not touching or moving any item.

He understood that Drew had experienced another shocking scene and would not remind her that their home, too, was now the scene of a crime, and nothing should have been touched or moved. No, he would not say that, but what he would do was leave the remaining rooms as they were to preserve the evidence. Then he called the authorities. They assured him someone would be there shortly.

While they waited for the police, Nonna made them all tea in the kettle that was dented but still usable. Chief Inspector Lewis and PC Claerk arrived shortly after tea was poured, and Drew related once more what she found when she arrived home from the funeral. Notes were taken, the rooms surveyed and photographed, questions asked again for clarification—did they have any idea who would want to do this? More notes were taken, then hands were shaken all a,round before the officers left them to deal with the detritus.

"I'll build the fire up and then look for your big cat," said Granda as he walked outside, closing the damaged door behind him.

"Granda is looking to have a last word with Chief Inspector Lewis, and while he does so, we will go to your room, dear, and put it all back together as best we can." Drew agreed, and after a tight hug, she and Nonna entered the chaos of her bedroom.

Her beloved books Drew picked up first, giving them a brushing off to dispel any malintent left behind before carefully placing them back onto her shelves. She hated that they had been touched and mistreated by someone so despicable. She and Nonna finished clearing her floor, turned the ripped side of her mattress down, and made the bed with fresh linen.

"I'll help you put the rest of your things away," said Nonna.

Drew shook her head. "Thank you, but I'd rather go through them myself. You go on and have a rest."

Drew was a minimalist. She had no desire for items of no use lying about in her space, so, other than her toiletries and a few keepsakes, her room was always tidy and spare. Two of the few treasured items she did have were damaged. A small porcelain bowl Nonna had given her for her birthday one year, in which she kept treasured trinkets found along the shore, was chipped, and the beautiful brown tortoise shell hand mirror belonging to her mother was now cracked. She gazed into the glass with a momentary hollow feeling, then continued sorting through the chaos. The top to the luminous cut crystal perfume bottle Serena had gifted her last Christmas was missing, but she eventually found it under her bureau, and at least that was unbroken.

The top drawer of her bureau was halfway out. The wooden box she kept her mother's treasured fountain pen collection in had been emptied, and the pens were scattered about what few belongings were left in the drawer. With a moan of dismay, Drew saw only three of the four pens were there. She looked everywhere in the room, but the beautiful blue Waterford pen was nowhere to be found. Tears stinging her eyes, she finished putting her room back together as well as could be, but it still held the unsettled energy of the intruder.

Both grief and anger welled up in her soul. She wondered how she would be able to sleep there tonight. How any of them would. She couldn't help thinking that what she was living in the moment could have been taken directly from a scene in one of her prized mystery novels. Reading about murder, funerals and break-ins was much more tolerable than living it. Despite the damp fall night, she opened her bedroom window wide to cleanse her space of the defiled air inside. She lingered in front of the window, looking out at the black sky, and took deep breaths of the cold as she sent a prayer off to Saint Charlotte to protect Vesuvi.

Drew went to find Nonna and found her on the sofa, looking completely done in. "Should we do your room now, before dinner, and then you won't have to do it later?" said Drew, in an effort to calm herself by continuing to put some order to the place.

"I think I need to sit just a moment more, and then we should eat. Your granda and I can do our room later, together. Let's finish setting this room to rights and then I can start a kettle and get us fed."

"You stay on the sofa, Nonna, and just rest as I do the tidying." Drew quickly gathered up all the strewn papers, turned the two chairs and tables upright, and placed the lamps back where they belonged. She stepped back to look at the room. It was the least disturbed, as it was mostly large pieces of furniture, and looked nearly the same as this morning.

Drew helped Nonna up, and taking her arm, they walked together to the kitchen where Granda had a roaring fire going. The warmth enveloped them as they stood arm in arm before the flames, looking about the familiar room now tainted by violence.

Granda had just finished squaring the door and closing it for the night. "I'll fix it properly tomorrow," he said. "I'll just take another a look about to see if there's anything else amiss."

Nonna put the kettle on and set a pot on the cooker to reheat the remains of yesterday's dinner while Drew gathered the last broken remains of the day. Three more chipped or cracked plates and three cups in a likewise condition were added to what she had already set on the table. The bare counters and empty shelves again gave evidence of all that had been lost. Along with the old familiar plates and dishes, the well-loved stoneware bowls for mixing and serving, the milk jug, the small stores of rationed flour, sugar, butter and spices, dried pasta and yesterday's bread were also gone. Granda had put the utensils—knives, forks, spoons, and ladles and such—back into the drawers. The silverware and two bowls and platters were the sole survivors of the devastation.

"They had the gall to take the bacon with them! Other than what was damaged and destroyed, I see nothing other than food that was taken from the house," said Granda coming back into the kitchen and giving both his wife and granddaughter reassuring hugs. "Sit down, both of you, and I will serve dinner. But first, I'll pour tea. There is still some in the tin."

A wave of weariness passed through the women as they sat at the table. Howard poured the tea, saying, "I'm sorry, Drew. I didn't find Vesuvi outside. I'm sure he's hiding close by, waiting for a time to come back. He will not have gone far."

"My only worry is that he was taken by whoever did all of this," said Drew, sweeping her arms towards all the rooms, her hands saying more than her words. "But I agree, that cat is a survivor. I can feel him not too far away, scared but alive."

"I feel him close by as well," said Nonna, giving Drew's hand a squeeze. "You'll find him tomorrow."

For some minutes, they silently drank their hot tea and ate the leftover pasta as a cold darkness fell against the windows of the kitchen. The bright fire from the hearth did nothing to dispel the feelings of vulnerability that hung in the air. It was late when they finished their meager dinner with their meager allotment of dishes, and they all agreed it was time to say goodnight.

Her grandparents still had their room to put in order, and she knew Granda would be the one to clear and set it to rights as Nonna gave him instructions along the way. Drew took some comfort in knowing Granda would walk the property one more time before he settled in for the night, for that was his routine, and tonight she knew he would be more vigilant than ever.

In the early hours before light, Drew was visited by a nightmare. She found herself standing on the side of the road looking expectantly to her right, seeing a long distance ahead. The light was fading to dusk when she suddenly saw the lights of a car moving into the curve of the roadway.

She knew it was her family on their way home, home to her. Suddenly the car swerved wildly as she watched the driver frantically trying to control the vehicle. She thought she could hear the screams of her mother as the car flew into the air and careened into the deep chasm below.

She watched, helpless, as explosion after explosion pierced her ears, flames appearing high above the road. She ran frantically towards the cliff. As she approached, she was overcome by the heat, and the thick smoke made her eyes smart. She was unable to catch her breath. A man suddenly appeared out of the smoke, his coat in flames all down his back, his arms flaying in a futile attempt to remove the burning garment from his body. She could not see his face, but she knew absolutely that it was her father. She had almost reached him, to save him, but when he raised his head and she saw the tortured face, it was the face of Alred Hughes. She continued towards the vicar, who turned round and round wildly, still trying to remove the flaming coat from himself. Drew watched in horror as he stepped too far and plummeted back down into the fiery chasm.

She woke then, panting and covered in perspiration. Unable to move, paralyzed with fear, she fought her way back from the horrible nightmare.

Trembling, she managed to sit up and turned on the small lamp beside her bed. She longed for the light of tomorrow; the dark held wild fears and worries. Lying still, she eventually slowed her breathing and calmed her racing heart. There was little she could do about her own past, but tomorrow was a day to get to the bottom of what was happening in the present. She knew the break-in was in some way connected to the death of the vicar. She knew what they had been looking for, but she didn't know why.

CHAPTER 11

SAINT CHARLOTTE –
MONDAY, 11 NOVEMBER

As she had the week before, Charlotte once again walked to the house where her father was murdered. The twists of smoke from the chimney told her the Davies girl was already there. She had no doubt that breakfast would be waiting as well.

Suspicious by nature, Charlotte, not for the first time, wondered at the young woman's audacity in inviting her to the vicarage. She didn't think the ladies of the church auxiliary would look kindly at Drew assuming she could invite and feed whomever she chose in a house owned by the church. But Charlotte jumped at the invitation and another opportunity, probably the last, to look through her father's effects. She felt more ready today to visit her father through his belongings.

"You're right on time, Charlotte," said Drew, opening the door before her guest could even knock. "Breakfast is ready and the tea is steeping. Come in and let's eat. I am always hungry, and I hope you are too." Drew was still reeling from the break-in of their cottage but knew she had to put on a brave face and get on with things. Chin up and all that. This morning she would accommodate Charlotte and then get this house packed up.

Charlotte followed Drew into the kitchen, placed her sensible brown coat over the back of the same chair she occupied a week ago, and sat down realizing she was indeed hungry. There was something about this young woman that put her at ease, which then put her increasingly on guard.

"It looks delicious, Drew. How very generous of you. I haven't had eggs in a while. And what is the delicious-smelling meat?"

"Isn't it lovely? To finally have fresh sausages after so many years of eating Glamorgans!" Drew brought the teapot to the table, adding to what already lay in wait for them: a bowl of golden scrambled eggs seasoned with fresh thyme, compliments of the family's hens; a platter of bangers, perfectly browned; thick slices of toasted bread; and one small jar of raspberry preserves that Drew and Nonna put up every year. Thank goodness the person or persons who broke in hadn't destroyed what they had laid up in the cellar. It didn't appear they even noticed it. Nonna's beautiful blue crock was thankfully spared, as she had taken it to the cellar before leaving for the funeral. Late carrots from the garden that Nonna pulled just that morning most likely saved her treasured Italian crockery.

Drew took a settling breath, bringing her thoughts back to the moment, and poured for Charlotte first. "I do hope the funeral wasn't too upsetting, Charlotte, especially Eira's reaction upon meeting you. I am sorry that she wasn't more . . . well, more welcoming."

Charlotte took up the cloth napkin lying beside her plate and gave it a fierce snap before placing it onto her lap. "I doubt anyone could have been less 'welcoming.' It was upsetting, to say the least, but I do understand the woman's shock. I also understand I will never have answers to lingering questions I was always too cowardly to ask the man before he died. I'd always told myself that with Mother's passing there would be time for me to seek out Alred and confront the man who laid waste to her life, to both our lives, really. The prospect of talking with Eira provided a faint hope that she would be willing to at least have a conversation. Perhaps shed some light on how he spent his life and if there were any other relatives besides the two of us and her son. And what a sad pair of women we are."

"Is that why you want to look through his effects again? Hoping to find answers?"

"Actually, hoping for anything that might give me insight into who and what he was about. Thus far, and after observing the lack of warmth from those attending his funeral and the brevity of the service, it is hard to comprehend why someone would murder a man who appeared to be such an unassuming person held in so little esteem. Does that not beg the question, 'What was he hiding from'?"

Having wondered this herself, Drew merely nodded and went about spreading jam on her toast. The raspberry was her favorite. "And have you had an opportunity to talk with the police? Could they give you any information regarding suspects, motive and perhaps whether a will had been found? Once you sought them out and told them who you were, I was very surprised they never sat you down and formally questioned you."

"I found the constable, the same one who attended the funeral, to be a man of few words, and the ones he did speak to me were curt and devoid of any information. He asked no questions of me and would answer no questions of mine regarding the investigation, saying when they knew something they would let me know. By far, you, your grandparents and the librarian, Lillian, are the kindest people I have come across in my time here in Mumbles.

"I did hope the police would be more interested in what happened and that my aunt Eira might want to at least have a civil conversation. And I am still hoping for some information regarding a will my father may have left or the name of a solicitor he would have used."

"I would think if your father did have a will or papers held by a solicitor that his sister would have that information. Are you interested enough in finding out that you might be willing to approach her again? After all, Charlotte, you are his daughter. And perhaps after another week, with some days gone by after the funeral, you will find her calmer and at least willing to meet with you in a more private setting, her home perhaps."

"I think she refuses to give any thought to the possibility that her brother could have fathered a bastard child, much less one suddenly appearing after an absence of forty years. Someone that I assume she never knew existed and therefore with no rights or claims upon a man who never claimed me as his own. I doubt very much that there is a will or other documents. And if they do exist, I do not believe I will ever see them."

Charlotte stared out the window, her eggs untouched on her plate. "I admit that I was hopeful that something might come to light, that perhaps he left something for my mother if she outlasted him, some token of atonement."

Drew had tucked eagerly into the food on her own plate. "And perhaps something for you as well, letting you know you *had* been in his thoughts?"

"Perhaps," sighed Charlotte. At last, she picked up her knife and fork and began eating.

A silence filled with unanswered and unasked questions lingered above the table and moved through the women's thoughts as they ate every bite of food on the table, albeit Drew consumed at least three-quarters of it. Since most of their rationed food was lost in the break-in, and it would be some days yet before they could queue up again for their weekly allotment, this breakfast was one she had looked forward to.

"More tea, Charlotte, or would you like to get to the study?"

"Yes, I am ready, and in more of a calm mindset than last week to scour the study and his bedroom. And Drew, thank you for the breakfast and conversation. The food was delicious. Your and your family's kindness is sincerely appreciated." Charlotte, appearing slightly overcome with emotion and therefore flustered, rose quickly and walked directly to the study.

Wanting to give her all the time she needed, Drew leisurely cleared the table and washed the dishes. She could hear Charlotte's quick steps as she entered the rooms her father would never see again.

When the kitchen was back in order and her supplies packed once again in the sack brought from home, Drew joined Charlotte in the study. Not seeing her but hearing a noise from about the desk, Drew was surprised to find the woman huddled underneath it, poking and prodding with a metal tool.

"Hoping to find a hidden cubby hole or a stuffed paper, Charlotte?"

"Well, I've found nothing of consequence in the drawers and files. So, here I find myself desperately seeking something that does not appear to exist. I think I will give it one more go under here before I give up."

Charlotte ran her hands with slow deliberation across all the smooth surfaces under the desk. Again, finding nothing that could be a compartment, drawer or a place to fit an envelope or paper, she then, leg by leg, began extricating her tall self out from under the desk. "And seeing the expression on your face, I find myself slightly embarrassed at my own act of desperation. I should have worn trousers. I notice they seem to be your choice of clothing rather than a skirt or dress."

"You are correct. Trousers are sensible and comfortable. Everyone has two legs, and we all need to have them free to do what we need and want to. I only wear skirts or dresses when I am going out or to an event, say a funeral or a celebration. The latter of which I much prefer."

"Well, I think you a wise young woman and one I may emulate during my stay here. But for today, in my cumbersome skirt, I have found nothing. And I agree with you. I would think a murdered man may have had something to hide, and who knows where it might be hidden."

Straightening her person and smoothing her attire, Charlotte once more opened every drawer. Her eyes and hands then scoured again the top and sides of the desk. "Nothing," she said, extremely disappointed. She should have known better than to think it could have been true.

With a last look at the curious framed picture of Saint Charlotte, she left the study to look through the drawers and wardrobe of her father's bedroom and bath. She opened the drawer in the small night table beside the bed and found bits and pieces of flotsam, a package of mints, and a well-thumbed copy of *The Common Book of Prayer*. Splaying through the pages, she found an old photo of her father as a young man. Beside him was a woman about the same age, and she assumed this to be Eira. She took the picture, closed the drawer, and went to the kitchen, where she found Drew reading.

Frustrated, Charlotte began taking up her belongings. "Thank you again for allowing me this time. I doubt my aunt Eira or the other ladies of the church would have been so accommodating. Oh, and speaking of Eira, I found this photo in my father's night table. I believe it to be him and his sister." Charlotte held the photo out to Drew. "Perhaps she would want it."

Drew took the photo and set it on the table, saying, "I'm glad it worked out for you to come today. Sorry that you didn't find anything helpful. And what will you do now?"

"I will think about what you said, of perhaps trying to speak to Eira. I doubt my request will be welcomed, but as they say, nothing ventured, nothing gained."

Drew walked Charlotte to the door and stood some time at the window, watching the tall woman walk back towards town to wherever she had her lodging. After Charlotte disappeared and Drew went to lock the door, something caught her eye at the edge of the door's small window. Getting a better view, she caught a brief glimpse of a man, the man in the bowler hat.

She surreptitiously watched him, pulling the edge of curtain back just enough to see him come through the gate and approach the steps, but he never climbed them to the door. He stood there looking at the house, then turned to the left and right of the property before leaving and walking in the same direction as Charlotte, back towards town. Had he followed her to the vicarage? Drew decided to pack quickly and leave the place herself.

• • • •

As Charlotte walked away from the vicar's house, she felt chilled to the bone. She knew it wasn't just the cold of the damp, overcast morning but a cold emptiness that encased her heart. She wrapped her coat more closely round her and quickened her pace as so many thoughts swirled through her mind.

After the death of her mother and then her father, she had assumed the constant bitter anger she felt would abate, and she would be left in peace. But now, with the man she thought she deplored gone from the world, all she felt was emptiness and an overwhelming fatigue. She felt she could lay down on this road and leave it all here, in this coastal village still ravaged by the war as she herself was ravaged by years of struggle and disappointment.

The long years of pushing and pulling to make something of herself, to prove she had worth, had taken a heavy toll. The chronic care of her mother, who was too lost in her singular world of despair to notice what went on around her, had taken years from Charlotte's own life and reinforced her mother's belief that neither of their lives had purpose.

Then why did Charlotte try so hard? The accomplishments of her profession gave her so little real satisfaction, no true sense of fulfillment, and certainly her ambition had brought her no close meaningful relationships—only the cold suspicion of jealous colleagues pretending allegiance. If they only knew her successes had brought her no joy.

She walked past the house where she had rented a room, past the tea room where she ate her one meal a day, past the homes of families where she watched children bounding out the doors towards school. She walked down to the water and onto the Mumbles pier. The inviting waves glided languidly towards shore as fishermen worked atop their moored boats, either having come back in from an early morning run or just about to set out. What must it be like to sail away on such a boat and know you could just keep going?

She never planned to stay after the funeral. She never really expected to find anything through conversations she might have had with the people at the reception. Nor did she expect to find any papers or possessions among her father's belongings that might shed light on the man he was and the father he wasn't. All she expected and hoped for was a release from the pain of rejection. Why hadn't his death brought that? She might have considered another course, had she known nothing was going to change. That even in his last days he was still the same person. She knew people never changed, so why had she allowed hope to blindside her?

There were still more than two months remaining of her sabbatical. No one expected her back in London until after the new year when the term began. She had no reason to return to the dark, empty house she had occupied with Mother. Perhaps, before the next term, now was the time to sell and move to a smaller place, or maybe even seek a new post at another school. Yes, selling the large house and putting much of that money away was indeed a good idea. Clearly, ridding herself of a house that never saw the light of joy was reason enough to leave. Could she begin again? She had no energy this day to even consider such an undertaking, but she did begin to feel the small spark of possibility.

Turning back round towards her lodging, Charlotte decided to let the woman from whom she rented know that she would like to keep the room for another month. She had nothing else to do, and perhaps something would yet turn up unexpectedly. She would, every so often, check in with the authorities for any news regarding her father's death, perhaps even seek out Eira again. She would truly enjoy spending more time at the charming and well-provisioned Mumbles library and continuing her daily walks along the shoreline, contemplating her future. So, even with her lifelong companion of caution whispering its concern in her ear, her heart won the day and quickened at the thought of such a bold decision. She decided to stay in Mumbles, to imagine and hope.

• • • •

The boxes Mara Roberts had given her she had stacked in the kitchen's pantry room. Drew pulled them all out and took three to the study. After looking once more out each window in the small house to ensure she was alone on the property, and checking to be sure both the front and kitchen doors were locked (thankfully the lock on the back door had been restored), she felt calmer and decided she wouldn't hurry.

She knew she needed to empty the contents of the larder and would start there, throwing out what few items remained. There was the nearly empty half-pint of milk, now smelling quite sour, which she took to the sink to empty and wash.

"Hello, are you there?" came a muffled, unfamiliar voice through the front door. Drew was so startled at the sudden intrusion she dropped the glass bottle into the sink, where it broke into large pieces. She heard the door open and the rustle of someone entering the house. On guard, Drew picked up the largest of the glass shards, held it behind her back and walked slowly towards the front door. "Who's there?" she called, before catching sight of the man standing in the sitting room. "What are you doing here?"

"It's Eira's son, Jac. I have my mam's key and let myself in. Didn't mean to scare you."

"Of course you scared me! Coming into a locked house where you knew someone was. What do you think you are doing?"

"Mam sent me over to see if you needed any help packing up. Mara told her you would be here, and I'm to see if you need anything, like more boxes."

"No, I don't need more boxes and I don't need any help. I'm almost finished. My granda and I will deal with the boxes as Mara instructed. Now you need to leave so I can finish my work. I don't mean to be rude, but I don't appreciate you coming into the house unannounced, key or no key." Although she'd not met Jac before the funeral, there was something about him that set her wrong. His aura gave off an intensity that was unsettling. She was extremely uncomfortable being alone with him in the vicar's house.

"Well, rude you are, girly. We only meant to help." He took two steps towards the door, then turned abruptly. "And whatever is left here now belongs to our family, Mam and me. Everything better be all neat and together, everything there. You understand? Mam won't be too happy to find it any other way." Throwing Drew a menacing look, he slammed the door and was gone.

Drew quickly locked the door, knowing it was for naught but needing to do it, nonetheless. Then she took one of the kitchen chairs and wedged it tight under the doorknob. She did the same at the kitchen door. She thought about calling Granda to help finish the packing with her, but she didn't want to appear frightened or foolish.

She stood against the kitchen sink and tried to slow her breathing and her racing heart. She resolved again to take her time packing up the study; she would look at every paper before sorting them into piles and placing them in the boxes. Maybe Charlotte had missed something.

She cleaned up the broken glass and finished in the kitchen. Next, she moved to the bathroom, emptying into the first box the few bottles and jars in the small cabinet over the sink. Hesitating, she wondered if the comb and yellowed dentures would be wanted by anyone. But in it all went, along with the bar of half-used soap, the dingy towel, and even the plunger beside the toilet.

Next, she packed up the vicar's small bedroom. She was glad the bloody linens and mattress had been removed along with the body. Looking about the room, the only thing dispelling the emptiness was a framed pastural print hanging on one of the walls. She opened the narrow wardrobe and removed what few clothes there were, including what she assumed were his formal clerical vestments. There were also two pairs of black shoes and a pair of brown boots. The dresser drawers held a small but tidy cache of folded shirts, underwear and socks. She realized that the women's auxiliary must have done his laundry.

Last, she went to the nightstand's single drawer. Inside was the lone dog-eared copy of *The Common Book of Prayer* where Charlotte must have found the photo. Rather than putting the missile into the box, Drew kept it aside, thinking it might, along with the photo, have some significance for Eira.

The study contained what would fill most of the remaining boxes. Going through the stacks of papers and files, Drew found nothing of a personal nature or anything that seemed related in any way to Charlotte or any family he may have had. After the desktop and drawers were cleared, she walked over to the picture of Saint Charlotte, still hanging on the wall between the windows. There must have been some intention on the vicar's part to have hung a picture of this godly woman, his daughter's namesake. Perhaps this was his singular gesture of atonement, a constant guilty reminder of the daughter cast off and rejected.

Trying to remove the frame from the wall, she found it nailed securely at both the top and bottom. She had often seen a red-rusted toolbox in the pantry and went to get it. There must be something inside to pry the frame from the wall. "Hooray!" Drew said aloud, after quickly finding a flat-tipped screwdriver. "The perfect thing!" She returned to the study and forced the tool between the frame and wall, prying it loose until it broke free.

She sat down on the vicar's large desk chair and studied the picture in her hands. The frame was approximately 25 cm by 33 cm and made of dark polished wood about two fingers in width. Both the print and the frame appeared very old. Some of the print on the picture, including what she assumed was a Latin inscription, was faded and difficult to read.

The back of the frame was covered by brown paper with no tears or cuts, and oddly, it did not appear old. Running her hands across the paper, she felt a bulge. Something was behind the backing. It seemed the Vicar Hughes may have left something in trust with Saint Charlotte.

With a great sigh, Drew mused aloud, "And what am I to do with this? I could just hang it back on the wall or consign it to a box along with the other leftovers of a bereft life. But of course, we are past that now."

What if this is important and not meant to be just some remnant to be piled together with other meaningless papers, never to be looked at again, she thought. I could assume it was for Charlotte and pass it on to her, but I doubt that would be wise, not knowing if it was indeed intended for her. Of course, I could give it to the officers, as it might shed light on the murder, but that seemed far-fetched, and how would I explain my taking it in the first place? I just feel that it was kept with Saint Charlotte for another Charlotte.

Drew laid the picture upside down on the desk. Using the letter opener she found in the top drawer, she carefully removed a portion of the paper from the back of the frame, revealing the corner of an envelope. She slid it out slowly and was not surprised to read the name of the recipient written in a clear hand: *To my daughter, Charlotte*. She carefully replaced the envelope behind the brown paper, then tucked the photo of Alred and Eira into his prayer book and put both into her leather satchel.

In less than an hour, Drew had packed away all the items from the vicar's house and moved all the boxes to the front door. At the last minute, she took the picture hanging in the bedroom and hung it where Saint Charlotte previously resided.

She removed the chairs out from under the doorknobs and returned them to the table, then walked the empty rooms once more before leaving, assuring herself her job was completed, that the house was clean and truly empty of all that remained of Alred Hughes.

Drew never saw the man in the bowler hat watching her as she climbed aboard her bicycle and headed home.

CHAPTER 12

LOST AND FOUND – TUESDAY, 12 NOVEMBER

In the half-light of morning, Drew woke with a sure premonition that Vesuvi was ready to be found. She felt him close by and ready to come inside. She dressed quickly and quietly left the house to walk the grounds round the cottage, looking in every small nook and cranny she came across. She began her search at Granda's large shed, where he had his workspace and a grand assortment of tools, and any number of hidey holes a cat could crawl into and disappear. But when she reached the door, she found the lock secure and the windows closed.

The lean-to greenhouse against the south wall of the shed included a walled off area that was the chicken coop, where more than a dozen clucking birds greeted her. Beyond that a narrow door opened into the greenhouse, where elevated wooden frames were filled with soil and chicken manure, prepared and waiting for spring. Nonna and Drew would plant seeds and small vegetable starts along with the large variety of herbs they grew year-round. The exterior greenhouse door was open wide enough for a large cat to enter and find safety.

"Vesuvi? Vesuviiii." Drew got down on hands and knees and crawled along the floor, looking below the planter boxes, where an assortment of pots and garden implements were stored. "Vesuvi, my great friend, if you are here, please let me know, and I will take you back into the house where there is warm milk and an even warmer bed for you. Not to mention a nice brushing and ear rubbing."

Did she hear a faint meow? Quickly crawling to the opposite corner and looking into the dark spaces, she glimpsed his big green eyes. That was all she saw of him but that was all she needed to know he was alive. She slowly sat down, wrapped her arms round her knees and continued talking in a quiet voice. She could feel his fear and hesitancy, even with her. What had they done to him?

"Vesuvi, can you please come out now? I really don't want to crawl under there and take you from your hidey-hole, but I will if you won't or cannot come to me."

"*Meow*," Vesuvi replied as Drew saw him struggle to his feet and limp towards her. With tears in her eyes, she gently lifted him onto her lap and sat with him in that half-light of morning. He had mud matted into his fur and smelled of fear and pain. She saw he no longer wore his woven collar with the too-large bell. Her suspicions confirmed, she was relieved she had the foresight to remove the keys and replace them with spare ones she found in the everything drawer in the kitchen.

"It's alright, my friend. We'll go home now and make it all better. I am so sorry you had to suffer cruel fools. You are brave and cunning."

Drew rose to her feet with the big cat held gently against her and walked back into the kitchen. Granda was sitting at the table reading his papers, and Nonna stood at the cooker making breakfast.

"Look who I found in the greenhouse." Vesuvi meowed again in greeting and letting Drew know he, too, was hungry. Probably hungrier and certainly dirtier than he had ever been.

"I'll warm some milk, dear, and we'll have a good look at him. He smells as though he has been mistreated," said Nonna.

"He is definitely injured. His left back leg is, and his collar, along with the bell, has been taken from his neck. I believe whoever broke into our home found what they were looking for."

Granda looked up from his newspaper, glancing from Drew to the wounded animal, her words immediately catching his attention. "And what would that have been, Drew Girl?"

"Two keys, Granda. Hidden, presumably by the vicar, in that large bell that was on his collar. It was so large and whatever was inside made such an unusual racket that it made me wonder. Not typical of a tinkling bell a cat would wear. A few days ago, before the funeral, I took the bell off and found keys inside."

Nonna placed the saucer of warm milk on the floor, and Drew set Vesuvi down in front of it. The cat slowly lapped it, taking a cautious swallow, and waited a few seconds before taking another drink. She wondered how much strength was used when whoever broke in forced the collar from his neck. No wonder his meows were feeble. His throat was hurt as well.

"And where are the keys you took from the bell? I would like to see them." Granda had that look on his face Drew knew so well: he was behaving calmly but was frustrated, wondering why she had not told him all of this before now.

Drew gave Vesuvi a light stroke along his back before getting up and going to her room for her satchel. "I put them in here, thinking they would be safe until I spoke to you. There hasn't been time to show you, Granda, really." She laid the keys on the table in front of him. He picked each one up in turn, examining them closely with a look of recognition on his face.

Drew sat down in her usual chair and reached down with a reassuring hand on Vesuvi, saying, "I think one key is to a locker at the train station. The number has been filed off, but I plan to find the locker it fits. Would you not agree, Granda?"

"Ie, it's from one of our lockers all right. The other key is too small to open a house or building, and it isn't an automobile key or for some other vehicle." After a pause, Howard added, "But I think it's used to operate some type of small machine. It looks familiar. I think it may be for a military-issue radio."

"But why would anyone need such a key now? And why hide it? The war is over."

"The war on the battlefields of Europe is over, but conflicts rage on and secrets abound. Secrets full of information people in high places are always looking to find."

"Speaking of secrets, tomorrow I'm going back to the vicarage, Granda.

I have the boxes packed with the vicar's papers and personal items. Mara instructed me to take them to the church, and I was going to ask you to drive me over and together we can load them. There is still one place in the house I think no one has thought to inspect. I was hoping before we left the vicarage you could see what you think as well.

"And also, while I was there packing up, Eira Hughes's son, Jac, used his mother's key and scared the life out of me. He let himself into the house! Said he knew I would be there and that his mam sent him to see if he could be of help. But I think his motivation was to scare and intimidate me. He made a point of letting me know that everything in the house was theirs, and I had better be sure it all went into the boxes."

Granda looked up at Drew with both concern and amazement, wondering who this young woman was and was she truly becoming a sleuth much like himself. "Alright, you have certainly sparked my curiosity. We can go early this afternoon. We'll leave the station about one and look round the vicarage, then drop the boxes off at the church."

As if knowing she was needed, Serena appeared at the door, knocking lightly and letting herself in. "I smelled breakfast all the way from my house. Along with the sense that a nurse is needed. Who should I be tending to this morning?"

Serena, Naomi's dearest friend and Drew's godmother, was also from Italy and had served as a nurse during the Great War. She was a woman of some height, with black hair generously accented by silver gray pulled up onto her head, and her bright hazel eyes and lovely olive complexion remained unlined and youthful. Her physical appearance reflected her young-at-heart spirit and a countenance radiating a subdued joy that filled any room with a bright energy.

With a nod, Granda handed the keys back to Drew, which she carefully placed into her satchel. Taking a collective breath, they all refocused on Vesuvi.

Drew picked him up and told Serena all about finding him in the greenhouse. "He must have either escaped after his collar was forcibly removed or been thrown outside when the house was broken into and hid in the lean-to. His left rear leg seems injured, hopefully not broken, and he seems to have difficulty swallowing."

"Well, let's take a look at your big fellow. Put him on the table so I can examine him." Vesuvi laid down on the table, allowing Serena to run her hands across his body. Her fingers came to rest on his leg, palpating the tissue and joints. Vesuvi let out a hiss and a low growl, letting Serena know she had found the source of the pain.

"Hold him steady, Drew. I need to determine if the joint is out of place or it's just a sprain." Drew held the big cat a little tighter as Serena felt the joint once more, followed by a loud protest.

"The area around the joint is definitely swollen, and I do think it is from trauma, as though he has been kicked hard. But I don't think there is any break or that it is out of the socket. But it must hurt a great deal and will probably take a couple weeks to heal. He needs rest, food and lots of your love, Drew."

"And his throat seems sore also. I think he is having trouble swallowing."

Again, Serena placed her skilled hands on Vesuvi and gently felt under his neck. He tried to pull away, but Drew held him tight.

"There is some swelling there. This poor animal has been badly abused. Has there been any news regarding who might have broken in and why?"

Granda responded, saying, "We believe the cat was injured by whoever ransacked the house. And as to any updates about the break-in, the constables say they have no leads and no witnesses and are still looking for the brute."

"I found something else at the vicarage that I need to show you," said Drew, walking over to her satchel. She pulled the framed picture from her bag and laid it on the table for all to see. "This faded picture of a saint named Charlotte. The framed Saint Charlotte was nailed soundly to the wall behind the vicar's desk in his study." Turning the picture over, Drew showed them the slit she had made in the paper, then lifted out the envelope that was clearly addressed to Charlotte Parkinson Hughes.

"It's obvious the vicar intended this to be found and given to Charlotte. I see no reason that it be kept from her. No reason to turn it over to the police but rather it be given directly to her. What a clever place to hide a note for her, inside the frame of her namesake."

After examining the picture and the envelope, Granda handed both back to Drew. "Put these back into your satchel along with the keys, and you and I will think on it later. In the meantime, you are not to go anywhere near the vicarage unless you are in the company of another person. And no more pulling surprises out of that satchel of yours. Now then, let's get on with breakfast."

With that said, they took their places at the table, Vesuvi remaining on Drew's lap, as Nonna placed eggs, bread and jam on each person's plate. Serena had generously given them several of her own plates, cups and what bowls she could spare from her kitchen. All during the rationing she had shared her allotment of flour, coffee and tea each week, saying that since she ate with them almost as much as at her own home, it was only right. And, of course, it was true. Serena was indeed a part of Drew's family and often shared either dinner or breakfast with them, as she was this morning.

Nonna poured tea for herself and Serena as Granda poured coffee for himself and Drew. Nonna and Serena talked about what pasta they would make the next Friday and if between them they had the ingredients for the sauce. Drew kept one hand on Vesuvi as she ate, not tasting the food, her mind already at the vicarage. Looking at Granda, she saw that he, too, was somewhere else.

CHAPTER 13

BACKSTAIRS –
TUESDAY, 12 NOVEMBER

Breakfast finished, Howard and Drew left for the station in Granda's reliable old lorry with reassurances from Nonna and Serena that Vesuvi would be well taken care of while Drew was gone for the day. Drew's satchel was parked on her lap as Granda drove quickly down the lane, headed for Swansea, both lost in their own thoughts and trying to make sense of who and why someone would break into their home and take those keys.

"I agree," said Howard, pulling Drew from her thoughts, "that the message behind the picture does belong to Charlotte, but it may not be your place to be the one to give it to her."

"While that may be true, Granda, I also know Eira would most likely not find the envelope but rather throw the entire picture into the dust bin without giving it a second glance. It is more than obvious she has no kind intentions towards Charlotte, and if she did find the note, there would be no passing it on to her. I think it would be a great disservice not to give her the envelope. The note is for Charlotte, what she is longing to find: some message from her father."

Howard slowly nodded. "Well, I can't disagree. Since you found the picture and the envelope, it needs to be your decision as to what is done with it."

She answered with a nod, knowing Granda knew what her decision would be and was reassured knowing he would do the same.

Drew had never felt time pass as slowly as it did that morning. She reminded herself not to glance at the time so often, as it wouldn't pass any faster. She and Granda ate lunch quickly and left a little before one. Arriving at the vicarage, Howard pulled the lorry close along the front gate.

Drew stepped from the vehicle, saying, "Granda, stop for a moment and look up at the house. This is what I want to show you. The window at the top shows an upper floor, or at least an attic space, but there is no staircase inside the house. It has always perplexed me, but with the vicar sleeping I never dared try to figure it out. There is a wall between the kitchen and the bathroom where I think stairs still remain. When I knock on the wall, the sound is hollow and the wood seems thin."

Howard paused, looking up at the window. Nodding his agreement, he then walked through the gate as Drew unlocked the door. He stood for several minutes, surveying all that could be seen of the house from the entry way before stepping into the sitting room and walking to the wall Drew had indicated. The area was paneled in a dark wood, matching closely the trim round the doors of the other rooms, and it was of ample width to house a staircase. Howard tapped on the surface of the wood, listening to the hollow sound and then ran his fingers round the edges feeling for a latch or lever. Finding none, he turned to Drew. "This does appear to be a false wall, and behind it there must be a staircase. It has also been here a good many years. It shows some age."

"Why was it put up in the first place? The stairs behind it appear to be the only ones accessing the upper floor. I looked in all the other rooms but found no way he could have gone upstairs from any of them. But then I remembered the small storage room off the kitchen and found what could double for stairs. They're cleverly hidden in plain sight. Come see, Granda." Drew quickly led him to the pantry and stepped through to the back wall. Granda followed close behind, marveling again at Drew's deductive skills and smiling to himself.

"I found this when I went through the shelves packing up the boxes but didn't have time to investigate. But the more I thought about it, Granda, the more it made sense."

Howard watched as Drew removed jars, bowls, a toolkit and boxes from a narrow set of shelves that began at the height of her knees and rose almost to the ceiling. "See? I think it's a cleverly disguised ladder, and I also think that is a panel at the top that opens into a room above."

Still smiling, Howard said, "Well, let's find out, Detective Davies. Since you found the ladder, you go first, and I'll bring up the rear."

Drew smiled back, nodded, and placed her foot on the first rung, making sure it was sturdy enough to hold her weight. She felt tingles of anticipation as she steadily climbed to what she believed to be the vicar's hidden passageway to whatever he wanted to hide.

Drew was tall, taller than the vicar had been, and she stopped several rungs from the top and pushed against a white panel of wood. It rose up and she slowly slid it to the right before climbing the remainder of the way into the space. Howard followed quickly, and soon they both stood in what was a single large room.

Drew watched Granda as he stood silently looking round the room, just as he had done at home after the break-in and downstairs just now when he first entered the vicarage—standing on quiet alert taking stock of the space, touching nothing but taking in everything. Drew realized this posture, this careful analysis of surroundings and the situation, was something he must have done many times before in other circumstances. When there was time and opportunity, she would ask him many questions. For now, she followed his example and slowly took stock of the room.

The space was an open rectangle approximately 760 cm long and 500 cm wide. A large six-lite window faced south along the front of the house and a matching one faced east. Both windows were fitted with blinds to control the light. And provide privacy. There was a hearth on the east wall directly above the one in the sitting room below. It was clean and looked as though it had not been used in years. The room was sparse and neat and was obviously set up as an office of some kind.

Drew was eager to explore but forced herself to wait until Granda was ready. She focused now on the contents of the room. A large wooden desk and chair was placed in the center facing south, just slightly back towards the wall. Another chair was placed to the side, also facing the window. There was a gray two-drawer metal file cabinet at the other end of the desk that Drew wanted badly to run to and open. The surface of the desk was clear except for two machines and a leather-bound book that looked like a ledger of some sort. One machine was clearly a telegraph machine much like the one at the railway office. The other machine was larger, and Drew wasn't sure of its purpose but reasoned both were used by the vicar for activities that had nothing to do with the clergy.

After several minutes, Howard began to slowly move about the room, beginning to his right along the east wall behind the desk. "Don't touch or move anything, Drew, but follow me, looking at everything and keeping a memory of it. This is how information is acquired, by careful attention to detail."

Drew followed Granda, not stopping until they had made a complete walk round the outer perimeter of the space. Then he walked across the room to the windows. On this clear afternoon, and because the vicarage sat so high on the knoll, much of Bristol Channel could be seen—east towards Cardiff and west to the Irish Sea.

In front of the east window stood a telescope and beside it, on a small table, a pair of large binoculars. Howard touched neither but turned and walked back to the desk, looking intently at the machines.

"Drew, would you please hand me the larger of the two keys in your satchel?" He placed the key into the keyhole on the front of the machine, turned it and then a dial. Almost immediately white static filled the room. Drew realized it was indeed a radio of some sort. Howard listened for just a few seconds, then turned the dial and the radio went quiet.

He handed the key back to Drew and sighed. "Well, you have doubtless found what may shed some light on why Alred Hughes was murdered. But there is more here than just information regarding one man's death. In addition to letting the police know what we've found, the war office will also need to be notified. Both the teletype and the radio are military-issue equipment. But not ours. The key you found accesses wireless military communication machines— like this wireless short-wave radio. The field commanders wore the keys round their necks to prevent anyone else from using the equipment. When needed, the commander would use the key, and his communication aide would radio or send by code whatever the commander dictated. I think the vicar was involved in intelligence work that may not have been for the good of Britain, or if it was, the presence of German equipment could indicate he was involved in espionage. Always a risky endeavor."

Howard headed back to the makeshift ladder. "Good work, Drew. You have a great mind for deducing the unobvious. We leave all of this as it is and head over to the police. I'll ring the railway office from the phone downstairs and let them know we'll be in later."

Drew felt a tingling of excitement at Granda's words. First, because she had uncovered what could be important information and second, because she found great pride and pleasure in working with her grandfather. What a relief to finally have some clue as to why an unassuming vicar was killed in cold blood. And, of course, whoever broke into their house knew Vesuvi carried the keys, and most likely knew about this hidden room. The same person who killed the vicar could also have been looking for the keys. She was eager to get to the railway station and use the second key to open the locker.

Drew stood in front of the desk and scanned the room one last time. Glancing down, she noted a single page of writing, half hidden underneath the radio. She could read the date and time followed by a sentence written in dark print, as though the writer had pushed extremely hard on the pencil tip. Farther down the page, in neat cursive script, were numbers followed by sentences she could only half see. This writing was full of curlicues and flourishes that could only be produced by a fine hand using an ink pen. Drew turned away from the desk, the writing on the page forged in her mind as she followed Granda back down the ladder. While he made the phone call, she went again into the vicar's study to the place on the wall that had held the picture of Saint Charlotte of the Resurrection. She wondered if what they found today would somehow circle back round to Charlotte Parkinson Hughes.

CHAPTER 14

CONFRONTATION AT THE POLICE STATION – TUESDAY, 12 NOVEMBER

D rew nearly jumped from Granda's truck as he pulled up to the police station's entrance. He would meet her inside once he had parked. Noticing her rapid breathing and racing heart, she took some deep breaths and collected herself as she approached the front counter, where she found the same officer she had attempted to speak with at the funeral.

"Excuse me, sir. I need to report some information."

The officer slowly looked up at Drew, taking stock of her, then turned his shoulder epaulette towards her, showing his rank. "Can't you read my collar number? It's *Constable*," he said crossly. "Constable Swain." He looked down again and fiddled with a stack of papers.

Drew knew he was going to be as belligerent as he was previously. Taking another deep breath to tamp down her rising frustration, she began again. "Excuse me, Constable Swain. Who would I speak with regarding information that may be pertinent to the murder of the Vicar Hughes?"

"You're the same nosey girl that interrupted me at the funeral. I'll tell you again what I told you then. This is no concern of yours, missy, and you may as well leave. You'll not be wasting your time, nor mine."

Howard appeared at the counter just as Swain finished his dismissal of Drew. "Private Swain, I see you've met my granddaughter, Drew Davies."

Swain stood up so quickly his chair fell over backwards to the floor. "Sergeant Davies, sir! Sir, I was just about to assist her. What is it again you need, miss?" The words tumbled out of his mouth as he looked first at Howard and then at Drew with eyebrows raised, trying for a bright, enthusiastic expression.

"She won't be talking with you, Private. You were rudely addressing a public citizen and demonstrating you have no real interest in doing the job you were sworn to do. A job which, as you seem to need reminding, earns you a living from the taxes Miss Davies pays. Not much has changed with you, has it, Private Swain?"

"No, sir, I mean yes, sir. How can I help you, Sergeant?"

"You can tell Chief Inspector Lewis we are here to see him, immediately and in private."

Turning red, with sweat beads on his bald head, Swain saluted, swiftly turned about, tripping across the overturned chair, and walked quickly in the opposite direction, apparently in search of his superior.

Drew couldn't help but smile at the exchange as she turned to Granda. "Sergeant Davies, is it? Good thing I brought some heavy artillery with me."

Howard smiled as well but remained ramrod straight, waiting for the Chief Inspector while Drew reminded herself that she needed to find out more about this grandfather of hers.

Approaching with an equally formal posture as Howard, Chief Inspector Lewis quickly saluted and then heartily shook Howard's hand while extending a nod of acknowledgment to Drew. Constable Swain stood off to the side, silently listening, his bravado withered, replaced by an air of embarrassed compliance.

"Hello, Howard, good to see you. What's this about you having information regarding Alred Hughes?"

"I'll let my granddaughter, Drew, explain," said Howard. And Drew did so succinctly, describing the whereabouts of the upper room and its contents.

"Granda says the appropriate military authorities need to be contacted regarding the equipment and papers found in the room. I assume you will do that for us, Chief Inspector Lewis?"

"Ie, ie, we'll contact the proper authorities today and coordinate meeting them at the vicarage as soon as they can arrange it. And thank you, young lady, for your coming forward with such information."

"Of course," said Drew. She looked past him to Constable Swain. "And if I do have reason, now or in the future, to engage one of your officers, I would appreciate being treated with proper respect."

"Yes, I understand, and that will be remedied immediately," said Chief Inspector Lewis, looking from Drew to Howard and then finally to Constable Swain. "Is that understood, Swain?"

"Ie, ie. Understood, sir," said Swain, not looking at Drew and barely nodding at his superior.

Drew didn't have much reason to think the constable would change his rude ways but thought he most likely thrived on his role as a belligerent bully of the law. She knew his treatment of her, should they happen to meet again, would remain dismissive and caustic. She would be ready.

"*Diolch*, my granddaughter and I will be on our way. Again, we trust you will inform the military regarding the equipment found in the office as well as the papers. Let them know it seems sensitive in nature and may be important that they secure the office and its contents as soon as possible. And you need to know that Hughes's sister, Eira, still has a house key as would, most likely, someone from the Women's Church Auxiliary."

With that final remark, Howard saluted Chief Inspector Lewis, who immediately returned the gesture, acknowledging one's understanding of the other. Drew felt she had just witnessed an exchange both men had engaged in many times in the past. She was beginning to realize her granda was one of many men here in their village who had most likely served together in the Great War. That their bond appeared strong and one of quiet, long-standing allegiance one to another.

Back in the lorry, they sat for several moments before Granda spoke. "It's in their hands now, but I would be curious to know what it is Alred was up to. I think he may have been giving the Germans information about ship movements."

"And I also think that Eira may have played some part in it all. The writing on the papers definitely looked feminine. Hard to believe they may have had any dealings with the Germans."

"During desperate times people do desperate things for reasons known only to them."

They drove to the church and dropped the boxes where Mara had indicated, just inside the door on the west side of the building. They continued on to Swansea Station in silence. Drew was relieved to be back at her desk and tried to settle into her work, but her mind kept circling back to wondering what the vicar had been involved in, and did it have anything to do with his murder. Desperate times, indeed.

Drew had stowed her bicycle in the back of Howard's lorry and left at her usual time. It was dark when Howard locked the station office and set off for home. He called Naomi before he left, letting her know she and Drew could go ahead with dinner, as he was just leaving. She assured him they would wait. He relished the occasional late hours required of him, and on those evenings, he drove home slowly with only his thoughts for company.

Even more interesting than the room they found at the vicarage was Drew's interest and ability in finding what was hidden. It seemed a knack for sleuthing could be hereditary, passed from him to Marco and on to Drew. She had always been a curious, independent child, constantly asking questions and requiring of him more than easy answers. She would probe beyond the obvious to find what she wanted to understand, which she often found in her beloved books in her beloved library.

But unlike her father, she had a quiet resourcefulness, rather than being pig-headed and stubborn. Drew would take counsel and listen, and hopefully think carefully about consequences before making decisions or plotting a plan. At least, that is what Howard hoped she did in other life situations he had observed, and what she seemed to be doing regarding the vicar's murder and the break-in to their home.

Marco would often become frustrated and seek out action before clearing his mind and reasoning his way through to a logical solution. Even after so many years, Howard berated himself for not intervening more convincingly, more forcefully, as Marco became more and more entrenched in the complicated affairs of military espionage. His actions saved unknown lives but cost him, cost them all, his family. Despite Howard's experienced counsel, Marco lived life believing himself beyond reach, that his work was necessary and that he could always keep himself and his family safe. But Howard knew that in war and politics no one was safe.

Howard was approaching the Mumbles Pier and continued on Mumbles Road as it curved to the right. He always felt the presence, even in the dark, of the gun batteries still in place, the guns on Mumbles Hill above Bracelet Bay to his right and those on Mumbles Lighthouse Island out to his left, overlooking the Bristol Channel. These defenses, with their artillery and searchlights, had provided strategic outlooks throughout the years of the Second World War. The defenses had been staffed with manpower and gunpower and kept readied to enter into conflict, had it become necessary.

Mumbles proper was never directly targeted for destruction, but Swansea did not escape the bombs of the Luftwaffe. The first bombings occurred on 27 June 1940, and again for three days in February 1941, the Swansea Blitz, when thousands of German bombs and incendiary bombs were dropped on Swansea. The city was bombed more than 40 times between 1940 and 1943. Hundreds were killed and hundreds more injured. The scale of devastation to the town was staggering. The rail yards in Swansea were a part of the ruin and disrupted both passenger and freight traffic.

The railway companies, of which there were many in the United Kingdom, needed to be overhauled, reorganized, reconfigured, and updated in all respects. Necessary changes were coming, and Howard was ready to be a part of those post-war changes. He hoped there was a place, a position, in the coming post-war reconstruction of the railways that Drew would find challenging and fulfilling. As much as Naomi, he, too, wanted Drew to stay close to home. He owed her what he could never provide to his son: an ever watchful and protective eye.

That evening, after Naomi had gone to bed, Granda asked Drew to join him at the table for a cup of coffee. Drew sat down, the warmth radiating from the hearth easing her mind as well as her body.

"It has been quite the day, Drew Girl. You did well with the police today, held your ground and related clearly what needed to be reported. Although, I suspect that under your calm explanation of things you might well be quite shaken from it all."

Drew nodded and took a long drink from her cup. All day the vision of the vicar, dead and lying under his bloodied sheets, haunted her. She had wondered why now, after more than a week, the horror of it all appeared so vividly in her mind. The memory of her nightmare also remained vivid. She understood now how soldiers in the battlefields might come home injured in spirit as well as in body.

"Did you see many dead bodies in the wars, Granda?"

"Soldier or civilian, depending on where you were unlucky enough to find yourself, saw death every day for what seemed eternity. It never got easier, it never will, especially when they die violently at another's hand."

"I see it all, whether my eyes are open or closed, the look of surprised horror on the vicar's face. I truly hope I will not see it forever." Drew hadn't felt the need to share the terrifying nightmare with either of her grandparents.

"Eventually it will fade to memory, and the rough shock of it will end. And once the murderer is found, the distress of it will ease. But the fact of it will become a part of your life."

"I want to follow the progress of the investigation and find out as much information as we can. For my own interest in it all as well as for Charlotte. I know something, of course, as to how she feels. Losing a parent, even one estranged as she was from her father, is devastating. Maybe even more so because they were estranged."

"Ie, Drew Girl, you do know a great deal about loss. And so much loss all around us after these challenging years of war makes a death so close by even harder to come to terms with. You and Charlotte have a common bond, and I would think the two of you could become close friends. Especially since you tell me she loves books as much as you do!"

Drew smiled, rose from the table and kissed her beloved granda. She washed and dried her cup and bade him good night. Snuggled into her bed, she read a while, choosing not a mystery but her well-loved copy of *Pride and Prejudice*. She had her own mystery to dwell on.

CHAPTER 15

PIEROGIS AND SAM –
WEDNESDAY, 13 NOVEMBER

T wo portable food counters took center stage each day in the station lobby, providing food and diversion for both passengers and railway employees. Both counters made their homes in front of the station's lockers. One of the counters, the most popular, was owned and operated by a couple originally from Russia, Mr. and Mrs. Ivanov. Every day, they brought delicious foods from their home kitchen, filling the lobby with enticing and spicy aromas reminiscent, in Drew's mind, of romantic and mysterious places far from Mumbles. On any given day, people with no plans to ride a train also stopped in during lunch to purchase a tasty meal they either ate with a friend on one of the long wooden benches in the lobby or carried back to their home or place of work. Fridays were an especially busy day, both for train travel and for the Ivanovs' food counter. They proudly made their "world famous" Russian pierogis once a week, always putting some aside for Drew, Granda, and Sam and the other railwaymen that had standing orders.

Annabelle, the custodian, stuck her head in the office door, saying not too loudly, "Pierogis are here."

Granda handed Drew some small change. "Get us each two, Drew Girl."

Halfway through their lunch, Sam appeared bearing gifts. More pierogis. "I see I'm too late. You've already eaten."

"Never too late, Sam," said Howard. "Pull up a chair and join us. If you have enough, I could eat another."

"Thank you, sir, I have plenty—four more, in fact. Drew, would you like another one?"

Drew's mouth was full of the flavorful dumpling, so she just shook her head and waved a hand. Sam smiled as he watched her try and manage a bite so big he thought she might choke. Unwrapping his own pierogi, he didn't hesitate to take matching bites. He was extremely happy to once again be in this familiar place, the station office, with two of his favorite people, one of whom had barely spoken to him in two weeks. He hoped the enjoyment of the mouth-watering food had broken through her stubbornness and things could now go back to normal. Without asking again, he set another pierogi on Drew's desk. He knew she was always hungry and would easily eat another.

"You are deadheading back on Friday, Sam?" asked Howard.

"No, sir, I'm staying the weekend with my family. My sister's new baby arrived a week ago, and she insists I come and meet my namesake. Another boy, and this one they named Samuel. She says they are calling him 'Sammy.' I need to get there and put her straight on that account."

Sam grew up in London where his family still resided, a wonderfully warm and loving family comprised of his parents, one sister, her husband, and now two small boys. Drew often went to London with Sam, staying at his parents' large home, and it was always enjoyable.

They most often went together when it was Sam's every-Friday-morning run to London. Drew rode in the engine alongside him, blowing the whistle and sometimes working the instruments, as he taught her the mechanics of what it meant to be an engine driver. He said she was a natural. Drew's happiest times were there in the engine with Sam, flying along the rails to London to be a part of a family—a whole family.

Between bites, she glanced up at the young man, her best friend and maybe something more over the last year. He hadn't invited her to go to London with him this time, and although she realized it was because he knew she would have refused, she wished he would have at least asked. She understood, though. She had been surly and distant recently, and now she was reaping the consequences. His hurtful words, the murder and then the break-in at the cottage had all caused her to back away. With the tumult of emotions, her first instinct had been to put some distance between them, to protect herself from others seeing feelings she felt made her seem weak.

She didn't share deep feelings easily, but Sam was always someone she could talk with. She did not like this air of muted friendship and cautious regard between them and wanted to rectify it immediately. When she caught his eye, she gave him a sincere smile and a nod. "I hope you have a wonderful time with your family this weekend. Please give them my best regards. I'm sure little Sammy looks just like his namesake," she said with a teasing smile.

Sam, slightly taken aback and extremely relieved at hearing what was a typical lighthearted comment from Drew, smiled in return. "His name is Sam. Just Sam. And yes, I will give them your regards." He gave her a big smile, the one that always made her insides tumble.

Lunch was over and just Granda and Drew remained in the office. Drew said, "I arranged to meet Charlotte at the library today at four, to give her the picture and note. Hopefully it will bring her some closure. It would be terrible if the note spoke anything other than kindness."

"You really are kind to Charlotte, Drew Girl. That poor woman is fortunate to have you taking an interest in her."

Drew left the station at 3:45, arriving at the Mumbles library as heavy clouds turned the afternoon into cold shadows. She leaned her bike to the side of the building's entrance and pulled her coat close round her as she hurried to the front door. She loved the library. In Drew's estimation, it was the most beautiful building in Mumbles, and one where she spent at least an hour or two every week checking books in and out and sometimes settling into one of the cozy nooks and reading for a time. It was the perfect place to meet Charlotte.

Charlotte was waiting just inside at the main desk, talking with Lillian, the head librarian, in animated conversation accompanied by quiet laughter. "Good day, Drew," they said in unison with wide smiles.

"And a good day to the both of you. You sound as though you're engaged in library conspiracy."

"Well," said Lillian, "we might just be."

More laughter escaped the two women before Charlotte turned to Drew in a more serious tone. "Thank you so much for meeting me here. I didn't sleep much last night wondering what you had found."

"Let's find a quiet corner where we can talk," said Drew as Charlotte led the way into the library, the smell of polished wood and well-worn books helping ease their mutual nervousness. "It seems as though you know your way round the place now, and you and Lillian certainly appear to enjoy each other's company."

"Absolutely, on both counts! Libraries have always been a haven of pleasure for me and a solace from the turbulent times of the world. I was always glad my work at university required I do considerable research throughout the years in the campus's expansive library. I found myself spending much time there.

"This lovely library has already stolen my heart. And Lillian, I think, could become a dear friend. I help shelve books and tend the card catalogue a few hours each day, as they do seem to pile up quickly. She will have no help now that her assistant is pregnant and will soon quit her job to take care of her home and growing family. I enjoy spending time here reading and also helping Lillian. Purpose, you know. It gives me purpose each day."

"Yes, I completely understand your fondness for this place. I love it too, and enjoy nothing more than finding books to check out and then spending time here reading by one of the windows. I only wish Lillian served tea and biscuits on Saturday. Granda says my two passions are eating and reading, preferably both at the same time. And I can't say he's wrong," Drew said with a laugh.

Charlotte nodded and smiled as she spied two other people and not wanting to disturb them found chairs and a small table by a window some distance away, cozy and private, the lamp on the table already lit. Once settled, they sat in anticipation, Charlotte of what she was to learn and Drew of how Charlotte would respond to whatever it was she would find when reading the note.

"When we were at the vicarage having breakfast and after your look round, I finished packing up all your father's belongings. I found myself continually drawn to the framed picture of Saint Charlotte of the Resurrection on the wall in his study, and out of curiosity, I removed it and noticed the bulge behind the paper covering the back of it. I slit the paper far enough off to lift out what was hidden inside and found this envelope addressed to you." Drew held the envelope out to Charlotte.

Charlotte sat still, staring at the envelope for several seconds before slowly taking it, and then sat many more seconds looking incredulously at her name written in her father's own hand. Her fingers slowly stroked the letters as she sighed and finally looked up at Drew.

"Now that I have some evidence that he really did think of me, I am scared to death to open the note. It may contain everything I dread to hear."

"It may also be everything you hope to hear. Why don't I leave you alone and you can open it now or later," said Drew, rising from the chair.

Charlotte reached out and clasped Drew's hand. "Can you please stay with me as I read it? Not knowing what it might say, I'd rather not be alone. And you were, after all, the one who found it."

"Yes, of course." Resuming her seat, Drew gave Charlotte a reassuring smile. "I have all the time you need."

Sitting ramrod straight in her chair and giving a firm nod to Drew to steel herself against disappointment, Charlotte carefully lifted the flap of the envelope, taking from it a single sheet of white paper.

Dear Charlotte,

If you have found this letter, it is more than likely because I have passed from this earth.

The picture of Saint Charlotte reminded me every day that I had a daughter. Reminded me every day that my greatest sin and regret was denying your existence. Pride is man's greatest folly.

Whilst I realize that nothing will atone for my neglect, I want you to know that I followed your life as best I could. You are a woman of intellect and have forged an admirable academic career. Even in my shame, I was always proud of you.

I have a legally binding will which you will find hidden in a desk in the vicarage. The will states I have left you £30,000. You will find a key in the bell of my big cat's collar, which opens locker #7 in the Swansea railway station. Inside the locker is the key to my safe deposit box in the London bank named in the will and where you will find the only inheritance I can give you.

Whilst it cannot act as recompense for my lack of fatherly duty, it is a token to say that I have always missed your presence in my life.

Your father, Alred Hughes

Tears glistened in Charlotte's eyes as she handed Drew the letter. She found a handkerchief in her handbag and dabbed away tears of relief as Drew read the note and returned it to her.

"You know that I rescued your father's cat, and he now lives with us, don't you? I noticed some time ago that the bell round his neck was rather large and jangled with an odd noise for a bell. I removed it and found two keys, one of which is the locker key your father describes in his note.

"What puzzles me is how carefully both you and I examined your father's desk and found nothing there. Either someone came ahead of us and found the will—"

"Or it was never there," interrupted Charlotte. "He perhaps meant to leave it but then changed his mind and never did? Even if we never find it or it never existed in the first place, I do feel a sense of closure. However, I do not know if his note makes me feel worse, even more disappointed and angry knowing he showed interest in my life and never let me know. At any rate and for what it's worth, at least I have this. Thank you for bringing it to me, Drew."

"Of course! And why don't you take the picture and do with it what you like. If you meet me at the railway station tomorrow mid-morning, we can open the locker. Even though we'll then have the key to the safe deposit box, we still need the will to prove your inheritance and get the name of the bank in London. It will hopefully be signed by your father's solicitor also."

"I'll be there at eleven tomorrow morning. Do you think we could go to the vicarage again and scour the desk one more time?" said Charlotte, gathering her things.

Drew had not reminded Chief Inspector Lewis that she still had a house key, as she reasoned she was the one who found the upstairs room and was in no way a suspect in the murder. And she was also, according to Mara's instructions, to check on the vicarage weekly. "I don't see why not. I still have the house key, and Mara wants me to check the house every week until another vicar arrives." With that they walked to the library's exit, each going their own way with their own thoughts.

CHAPTER 16

PASTA FRIDAY –
FRIDAY, 15 NOVEMBER

One Friday a month, Serena would join Drew and Nonna for pasta making and dinner. Serena always brought the music, one of her own records of Italian songs, and Drew could hear the strains of a passionate tenor singing what she knew were words of love and longing even before she opened the front door.

Serena looked up from the table as Drew entered the kitchen. "*Buona sera*, Drew. Just in time for rolling and cutting."

Drew saw that the pasta board was floured, and a roll of dough sat squarely in the middle. She kissed Nonna and then Serena on both cheeks before gathering her great cat into her arms. "I see Vesuvi has been keeping a watchful eye on the goings on here till I arrived."

"Si, si, Vesuvi is an old Italian spirit, and he adores the love songs, as any good Italian would," replied Serena, waving Nonna's long mattarello in the air as she began crooning along with the music, serenading Vesuvi.

Nonna watched the play between the two women she loved best in the world, a broad smile on her face as the past, present and future joined together here each month.

Drew piled more wood onto the hearth, then went outside to gather another load.

"Our Drew becomes more lovely every time I see her. Is that young engine driver Samuel still smitten with her? Should I begin hoarding material for her wedding trousseau, Naomi?"

"Samuel? They seem to have been at odds with one another lately, or rather, I think Drew has been somewhat out of sorts with him. I think she is restless and wanting to figure out her place in the world."

"I would think her place is clear: beside that handsome young man with a good job from a good family."

"Times are different now, Serena. The war is over, and women who worked the factories and did the labor of men, especially the young women, are hoping they have more options than we did. Our aspirations were to escape the devastation, and how fortunate we were to find our good men and a good life with them here in Wales."

As always, and as she would forever, Serena bowed her head as she made the sign of the cross in memory of her late husband, Owain. "Si, I suppose it is too early for the wedding dress, but you know, I always keep my eye out for that special white fabric that will make Drew the most beautiful bride in all the world," she said, sweeping her arm wide for emphasis.

Drew came back into the kitchen, arms full, and deposited the logs on the floor with loud thumps. Vesuvi jumped from the chair and trotted over to investigate as she stacked the wood beside the fireplace.

Drew washed her hands and donned her apron. "And now, *donne adorabili*," she said, turning, "I am ready to make pasta. And what are we creating today?"

"Today, we make *zuppa di pollo*, so we will be making the tiny star-shaped *pastina*. And I have brought my cutter, so your job is to cut the pasta into the tiny star shapes as quick as we roll it. And, of course, to keep the music going and the fire roaring. *Capisci?*"

Drew waved the cutter in the air. "Si, si. I am ready!"

Naomi and Serena had met when they were young war brides. Howard and Owain had grown up with each other in Swansea, fast friends who entered the Great War as young volunteers, enlisting together on the same day. Both stationed in Italy, Howard was assigned to the railway battalion and met Naomi at a market during one of his rare layovers in her small village. Owain, assigned to the infantry, met Serena in a field hospital, where she served as a volunteer nurse and cared for him after a severe concussion and extensive shrapnel injuries. Both men had found the loves of their Welsh lives in Italy and, following the war, brought their brides home, where the women became immediate and fast friends.

The couples bought old stone cottages on adjacent properties of substantial size and restored them together, creating lives in Mumbles filled with hope, hard work and laughter. They also expected to fill their homes with beloved children, but that was not to be. Serena and Owain never had the children they longed for. Naomi and Howard's only child, Marco, became the other couple's godson, and they poured all their love into that boy.

Owain passed away the day before he turned fifty. Disease took him so quickly they all had little time to prepare their hearts for the loss. Once Serena pieced herself back together, she poured her energies into her dressmaking, a skill she learned from her mother. She set up shop in her home and filled her time making other women's dreams come true. Wedding dresses and trousseau ensembles became her specialty. Just as Nonna had brought her pasta board and mattarello, Serena left Italy with only her sewing machine and her craft. After living through the dark times of the Great War and caring for men who were often at death's door before they even arrived at her hospital, she never wanted to return to nursing.

"Drew, I see that both your and Vesuvi's auras are lovely today. You two seem quite aligned. Tell me again, please, why he chose to come live with you."

"During the time I cleaned the vicar's house and prepared his meals, Vesuvi was always there, and we quickly became friends. He would follow me round the small house, and we would chat as I went about my routine. He was always wonderful company, listening attentively to my thoughts and always offering helpful advice. I do feel he and I have been close friends for a very long time. Right, big fellow?" Drew bent and ran a hand down her cat's back, and he gave a loud *meow* in acknowledgment of all she said.

"I need to talk with you both about these auras the three of us see, the colors round people's bodies and the bands of light in different shades and widths," said Drew. "What am I to make of this, as it seems to be happening quite frequently? Especially if I pause to notice, although it can sometimes take me by surprise. For instance, when Jac Hughes let himself into the vicarage that day, his aura was so disturbing I'm still troubled by it. The day of the funeral both he and his mother had similar dark auras, but that was to be expected. But still, Jac's is stormy and threatening.

"Nonna, you say I saw auras when I was a young girl, that Serena saw them too, but neither my parents nor Granda ever saw them. Is it passed down in families, like from you to me? Because I also see these same auras with Vesuvi and have always sensed his strong connection with me. It makes me think that animals are more like us than different."

"Ah, how wonderful!" said Serena. "I love these times when we make our pasta together and can talk about such mysteries. We were hoping you would eventually ask more questions, and how exciting that the three of us share this rare gift." The two older women looked at each other and smiled in agreement before Serena turned again to Drew.

"To begin, all living things are alive with energy. It flows through us and around us, in a way much like I have come to understand electricity. You cannot see electricity moving through wires or cables, but you see what it creates, such as light and power. Auras are the energy surrounding people, and some people, like us, see this energy as bands of color. Have you ever experienced seeing the aura of someone you know who is generally upset or difficult most of the time and compared that with the aura of someone who displays a pleasant and calm nature?"

"Ie," Drew responded. "When I see a person's aura, especially when someone seems out of sorts, upset or angry as Jac was, or even if they seem sad, the colors alert me as to what they are feeling. I find I interact with them in a way that best suits their mood, such as remaining quiet and listening if they wish to talk. But when I see dark or stormy auras, I tend to move away from people. I don't see everyone's auras, and with some people I would rather not see theirs at all. I think it is sometimes better not to know what someone is feeling. Especially the people I care most about."

"Like Sam, for instance?" said Nonna with a gentle smile. "I, too, would often rather people keep their auras to themselves." All three nodded in mutual understanding and continued rolling and cutting the pasta. "As to where these gifts come from, and they are a gift to be sure, they do seem to be handed down. I have known men who had the ability, but I do think women tend to be more ethereal and open to these mysteries."

"You say it is a gift, Nonna, but for what reason, and what are we to do with what we see and understand?"

Nonna continued rolling as she answered. "Spiritual gifts come in many forms. For example, saints and physicians heal, nurses and angels comfort, and others see what is inside another's heart. That is our gift, to see the true nature of what another is feeling or experiencing. And what do we do with this knowledge? As you say, it causes us to think before we speak. To the hurting, we can offer a kind word or help; to those confused or seeking guidance, we can perhaps encourage them; and those whose auras are dark and even dangerous, we stay alert and away from them and hope they can find peace."

Drew took in their words, which made her want to understand this phenomenon in greater depth. Perhaps there was a book at the library that might explain more. She would check next time she was there. It was comforting to know that they all shared this same ability, and she knew she could always ask either one about whatever was on her mind.

The last of the afternoon sun shone through the windows of the kitchen, and it wasn't until the sky settled into the horizon that the three companions finished their task and could begin preparing dinner. Granda always brought home a special wine, Italian of course, for this monthly ritual that had taken place since the brides first came to Wales with their men. Drew always felt so privileged to be a part of the warm companionship of these beloved people. And now Vesuvi had joined them. All their auras shone in harmony that night.

CHAPTER 17

A WILL AND INVITATION – SATURDAY, 16 NOVEMBER

After several attempts to contact Charlotte by phoning her lodging, all of them unsuccessful, Drew made the decision to stop at the bed and breakfast to let her know they could meet at the vicarage this Saturday at nine a.m., rather than Monday. She reasoned this would constitute her weekly check on the empty vicarage to assure all was in order.

When she arrived at Charlotte's bed and breakfast, Mrs. Stable, the landlady, who was somewhat familiar to Drew as she had occasionally seen her about town, told her Charlotte was out and she did not know when she would return. That it was none of her business where her lodgers went about, and therefore, she could be of no help.

"If I might take a minute to write her a note, would you be so kind as to see she gets it?"

"I'll put it in her box, but whether she looks there or not is also none of my concern."

The woman was most unhelpful, but Drew was undeterred. She pulled pen and paper from her satchel and hastily scribbled a note to Charlotte, folded it and handed it to the woman. "Thank you for putting this in her box. The note is important, and if you see her, I would appreciate it if you would let her know Drew Davies left her a message."

"Honestly, you cannot expect me to remember such a thing when I am so busy with them all coming and going and wanting to eat at all hours. I make it clear when we eat and what we eat and there are no exceptions."

"How many guests do you have right now?" Drew asked innocently.

"Two, I have two. Miss Charlotte and a very rude gentleman from Scotland. Rude to the core."

"Well, rather than trouble you, why don't I just put the note in Charlotte's box myself, just in case, in your busyness, you forget."

"Absolutely not, young lady! No one goes round the other side of my desk. Just give me the note and hope it gets to your friend. I make no promises."

"Would you like it if Miss Charlotte extended her stay for another two weeks or more? If so, you need to be sure my note gets into her hands today. Otherwise, she may need to leave immediately, and you'll be left with only the rude Scot."

"That important is it, you say? She's a nice woman and a quiet guest. I like her kind. Fine then. I'll be sure she gets your note today." With that, the brash woman turned away quickly, sidling her short round body along behind her desk to a row of small wooden boxes wide enough for envelopes and room keys, and slipped Drew's note into box number four.

Once outside, Drew shook her head to shed the woman's dour energy and left for home. The brisk wind off the bay cleared her head as she wondered how people came to be so unpleasant, which Drew always equated with being unhappy with their lives. Charlotte seemed to like being there, and perhaps she got on well with the woman. For Charlotte's sake, she hoped that was the case.

That Saturday, Drew approached the vicarage just before ten and saw Charlotte already standing by the front door. Obviously, she got the note. This day, Charlotte wore trousers, sensible oxfords, and a short coat and gloves. But, because her deportment was now so familiar, Drew knew who it was long before she ever got close to the house. She pedaled faster and rode her bike round to the back and fished her house key out of her satchel as she walked to the front door.

"Hello, Charlotte! I now know that you are always on time and are very dependable when you have a place to be. I'm glad my note made it into your hands and that your landlady didn't forget to tell you."

"It was the first thing she said to me when I returned. She said it was urgent, and after I read it, she asked if I would be able to continue renting the room for the remaining two weeks. I assured her I was, curious as to what you had actually told her."

Drew looked nonchalant, saying, "Oh, she was so unaccommodating that I may have suggested that your continuing to stay was based on the information in my message."

Charlotte smiled at that and gave a light chuckle. "I can picture that exchange."

After closing the door and locking it behind them, both realized that it was as cold inside the house as outside, and they kept their coats and gloves on as they walked straight to the vicar's study.

"We'll be quick about this," said Drew. "You look under the desk again, and I'll go through the drawers and round the outside. If we find nothing, then we'll switch places and look again."

Charlotte, who had brought a torch with her, immediately dropped under the desk, switched on the light, and slowly traced all edges and surfaces of the underside. Drew did the same on the outside, going carefully through each drawer, examining every nook and cranny, top and bottom, looking for any buttons, levers or hidden places. They found nothing, switched roles and again came up empty. They even searched the chair and the lamp, but still nothing.

Drew dropped down into the vicar's chair and looked about the room. Assuming the vicar was telling the truth, the will was in a desk. What were they missing? A desk.

"Do you have the note from your father with you?"

"Yes, I carry it in my handbag." Charlotte found the note and handed it to Drew asking, "Why? Did you think of something?"

Drew unfolded the note and read the words again. "'I have a legally binding will, which you will find hidden in a desk in the vicarage.' Charlotte, stay here and let me know if anyone comes to the door. If they do, don't answer it. I'll be back shortly."

"But where are you going? I don't want to be left here alone."

"I'm not leaving the house, just going upstairs. It's a long story, and I'll tell you when I can. Just stay here, away from any windows, and I'll be back down soon."

Drew went to the pantry, where she found the laddered shelves still bare, and climbed to the upper room. The vicar was not talking about his study desk, his personal desk, but "a desk," the other desk in the house.

Drew couldn't tell if the police had inspected this room after she and Granda spoke with Chief Inspector Lewis. Nothing appeared disturbed. All looked exactly as she and Granda left it. Tugging her gloves more tightly onto her hands, she quickly went to the desk, pulled out the chair and got down to the floor to examine the underside. She found no compartments, no crevasses to hide an envelope and nothing taped to the bottom—nothing at all.

She crawled out and walked slowly round the desk, wondering if any of the drawers opened. The middle drawer was locked but the ones on the right-hand side opened, but there she found nothing. The same with the top left-hand drawer. Frustrated, she opened the bottom left-hand drawer and, as she had with the others, felt behind the drawer itself. A thrill of excitement passed through her as her fingers touched a small lever. When she pushed it, the back panel of the desk's frame slid open, revealing another space. Drew felt her aura flare. She was looking at an envelope addressed to Charlotte Parkinson Hughes. The will was indeed in a desk, just not the one they assumed.

After making sure all the drawers were closed and sliding the chair back under the desk, she scanned the room. There could be no sign of her having been there. She then hurried back down the ladder and found Charlotte waiting by the front door, anticipation in her eyes.

"And so? Did you find anything?"

Drew handed her the envelope. While Charlotte stared at the paper in astonishment, Drew took another look out the window, unable to keep the smile from her face. When she turned back, Charlotte had already opened the document and was reading it.

"My father . . . he left me £30,000! The will looks to be in order. It was witnessed and signed by a solicitor named William Sussex, Esq."

"William Sussex? The solicitor who signed the will is named William Sussex?" Surprised, Drew looked over Charlotte's shoulder, quickly skimming the paper.

"Why yes, is he familiar to you?"

"Yes, you might say he is and how very interesting. Charlotte, I would suggest that you not show this to anyone just now nor try to get in touch with Mr. Sussex. Let me speak with Granda to make sure you show this to the right people who can verify that the will is legal and in order. Then we can go from there."

"I don't understand, Drew. It all seems in order, and I would like to get this cleared up as soon as possible."

"You asked if I knew Mr. Sussex. While I don't actually know the man, I frequently saw him at the rail station as he traveled back and forth from London twice a month. Shortly before our home was broken into, Bowler Hat—that is what I call him because he always has such a hat on—was in my queue to buy his return ticket to London and demanded to know where the vicar's cat was. Had I seen the cat, and did I know if it was still at the vicarage. I honestly told him that I had not seen the cat at the vicarage and asked why he was asking me questions. He didn't respond, and I told him he was to either buy a ticket or get out of the queue. He quickly left the station. I saw him cross the street but didn't see where he went after that. I asked Granda if he could find out who the man was, and he was told his name was Sussex.

"Now what would he want with Vesuvi, other than to get the keys from inside the bell? And why would Mr. Sussex want those keys? And why has Mr. Sussex not come forward letting the authorities know your father had a will, witnessed and signed by him? So yes, Charlotte, I'm asking that you hold on to the will and say nothing about its existence until I can speak to Granda."

"Well, putting it that way, it does seem wise. Do you think this man had anything to do with my father's murder?"

"It is very unusual that he told no one about the will and was looking for the keys. It stands to reason he was after the will himself. But why?" Seeing darkness not far behind the day, Drew said, "It's time we left. I'll get my bicycle and then we'll walk together to your place before I go on home. Please stay close by the B and B or the library for now, and I'll be in touch."

Drew locked the door behind them, got her bike from around back and together in silence, each keeping to her own thoughts, they walked towards town. She needed to think and was glad she would have some time before Granda arrived home that evening.

Entering the cottage, Drew's eyes were drawn immediately to a thick envelope lying on the kitchen table. She set her leather bag on a chair, removed her gloves and picked up the envelope. The feel of the creamy velum stirred a sense of anticipation as well as surprise when Drew saw her name in fine script on the front. She opened it carefully. It was a note from Sam's mother, Kathleen Provens, written in the same elegant handwriting and on the same rich paper as the envelope.

Dear Drew,

We are having a few family members and friends over to celebrate the Holidays. We hope you can join us on the evening of Saturday, 9 December. Your room will be ready for you to stay as long as you care to visit. We sincerely look forward to your company.

Kind Regards,

Kathleen and Douglas

Smiling as she ran her fingers over the thick paper, Drew knew she would attend and would do so with Sam. His parents were some of her favorite people, and being in their home during the holidays, a time of celebration after these hard years and the events of the last weeks, was surely something to look forward to.

"There you are, my Drew Girl. I see you found your lovely invite," said Nonna as she came to give Drew a welcoming hug. "We received one as well. How kind of Samuel's parents to invite us to their home. Of course, we will not be attending, but it is always nice to be asked."

"And why wouldn't you and Granda come? Their home is so large, there are rooms enough for the three of us."

"Oh, ie, we have been there before. But Granda and I would rather be here. You know he will have to work, and we really have no longing to travel to London. But what I am more than excited about is planning what you will wear. I've already spoken with Serena, and she is bringing some fabric over for you to look at."

"This invitation just arrived! How could you and she be plotting my wardrobe so quickly?"

A sharp knock sounded at the door, followed by Serena stepping through to the kitchen, her arms piled high with fabric which she laid atop the bare kitchen table.

"How about a cup of tea, Naomi," said Serena, giving each woman a quick hug, "and then let's get down to business."

Drew didn't know whether to be offended or flattered by the attention of these two. But she did know that tea sounded wonderful, and thinking of a new dress after so many years of nothing but mended trousers and threadbare blouses sounded equally welcome.

"I brought several different fabrics, Drew, but truly there is only one that is to become your holiday dress."

Serena picked up a large swath of deep blue velvet and lifted it to Drew's body. Running her hands along the fabric, Drew felt a charge of emotion. How could the sensation of cloth make her feel so delighted? The velvet was thick and soft. She wanted to wrap herself in its richness and feel it covering all of her.

"This is so lovely, Serena. I have never felt such material before. Wherever did you come by this?"

"It has been rolled in linen and kept in a cedar trunk amongst other fine fabrics for so many years I have lost count. How thrilling to know it was waiting for you, darling girl, and for a holiday party to lift all our spirits. I am thinking of a tea-length dress, scoop neck and three-quarter sleeves. I have a rope of small rhinestones to sew at the neckline and along the edges of the sleeves. A simple, elegant gown highlighting your blue eyes and copper curls."

"The dress sounds so beautiful. I cannot thank you enough for being willing to sew this up for me. Of course, I will pay you for both the fabric and your time."

"*Senza senso*, nonsense! It is my pleasure. I have been wondering when this beautiful fabric would find its place, whom it would choose to grace. Well, actually, I always knew it was for you. And now my fingers are itching to create!"

Picking up another length of material from the stack on the table, Serena said, "And next, a gray wool felt." She held it up to show them. "This will make a perfect winter coat. Again, a simple style that you can wear for many years, with deep pockets and a nice collar. And this piece," she said, unfolding the last of the fabrics, a length of lightweight brown worsted wool. "This piece will make a lovely pair of trousers, which will be perfect for daytime in the city. We all know how fond you are of trousers, dear."

Nonna chimed in then, "And I have a fine ivory silk blouse that will work perfectly with the trousers. You will be the fairest at the ball, my girl."

Feeling overwhelmed, tears sparkling her deep blue eyes, Drew pulled them both into her embrace. "You are truly my fairy godmothers. I have no words to thank you. Your kindnesses have also made me very hungry, so now I will fix us something to eat . . . and more tea." Drew hurriedly wiped the tears from her eyes and busied herself in the kitchen as the women chattered on.

Two weeks later, the three gathered in the sitting room to fit Drew in the fine clothes Serena had sewn.

"I have taken long stitches at the waist and bust to allow for alterations, and I will pin the hems after you have the dress and trousers on."

Drew stepped into the trousers, the fine wool sliding smoothly up her long legs. There were front pleats and a narrow waistband with a zip-and-button closure. The fit was perfect.

"We will not put a cuff on the trousers but keep the leg straight to allow for a timeless style," said Serena, kneeling on the floor in front of Drew and talking through a mouth full of straight pins. "Oh, how lovely it is to once again be sewing, and how very wonderful that it is for you, my beloved goddaughter."

Nonna had brought out the ivory silk blouse, and Drew slipped it on carefully as Serena continued to pin, instructing Drew when to turn and when to stand still. Nonna buttoned up the front of the blouse, the delicate round buttons covered with the same ivory silk. The blouse had a narrow, rounded collar, and Nonna left the top button undone to allow the material to drape softly across Drew's collar bones.

When Serena had all the pins in place, she turned Drew to the mirror in the hall. What Drew saw was a tall young woman dressed for someplace to be. She stood a little straighter, running her hands along the silk of the blouse and down over the fine wool of the trousers. "It is all lovely. I will be afraid to eat anything for fear of spoiling the fabric. I'll need an apron to wear at all times!"

The women laughed and told Drew to undress again. She did, carefully laying the clothes across the sofa after relocating Vesuvi, who had been watching everything with interest from a plush cushion.

The blue velvet dress was then lifted slowly over Drew's head. Her arms glided through the sleeves, and the dress fell smoothly over her body, the rich fabric resting into her curves. Small buttons, running from the neckline to her lower back, fit into delicate velvet loops and were done up by Serena.

"And her hair, Naomi. Can you bring some combs and pins? Let us put her curls up."

"Sit down, Drew, and let me do your hair," instructed Nonna, returning from her bedroom with two wide tortoise shell combs and a small box of bobby pins.

After several minutes of conferring with one another, the women had Drew's copper curls crowned atop her head. Soft ringlets framing her face created a perfect symmetry.

"*Bellissima*," sighed Nonna as Serena once again turned Drew towards the mirror. The dress was breathtaking. It flattered Drew's figure perfectly, the velvet shimmering in soft waves all along the length of her. The waist was fitted and the skirt slightly flared, the hem finding its finish between knee and ankle. The delicate rhinestones along the neck and around the edges of the sleeves gave the dress an understated elegance. Drew felt transformed as she gazed at the reflection of the copper-haired, blue-eyed woman in the most beautiful dress ever created and echoed Nonna's sigh of *bellissima*. She took each woman in turn and danced them round the room, loudly humming an Italian aria as they all laughed, delighted at the outcome.

"And for the finale," said Serena, picking up the coat of gray wool and sliding it carefully over the dress, "your coat, *giovane donna!*"

Drew hugged the thick fabric around her body, looking into the mirror this way and that. She felt an overwhelming sense of gratitude. In a burst of joyful energy, Drew picked up Vesuvi and danced him round the room, too, all thoughts of wills, bowler hats and murder far from her mind.

CHAPTER 18

PINE GROVE MANOR –
SATURDAY, 7 DECEMBER

Drew and Sam stood on the platform beside the 8:00 to London. "Since I'll be in the engine with you, I'll just lay my clothes bag out across the luggage rails above seats no one is occupying," said Drew. "It and my small case will be fine there."

"You know the train will be full of passengers, and to leave your new clothes stowed without you to watch them, unless you want them to disappear or have bags stacked on top of them, isn't the best idea. Maybe you should stay there and mind your clothes. Riding in the engine with me happens fairly regularly, so what's so special about today?"

Drew watched as passengers scurried to board and find seats, finally replying, "I haven't been to London since before V-E Day, in May. I know so much is in ruins and seeing the city high up from the engine cabin will show a truer state of things than looking out a coach window. Besides, it'll be difficult, the damage and all, and seeing it with a friend would be easier."

"Right. Well, I suppose we can give your bags to Fitz, and he can stow them in the brake van. It *is* difficult seeing the bombed-out buildings and people trying to go about their day amongst the rubble."

They took Drew's garment bag and her overnight case and quickly gave them to Fitzhugh, the guard, who reluctantly agreed to put them in his brake van at the rear of the train. Drew and Sam ran to the engine and climbed aboard. The fireman greeted them with "Let's get rolling!" just before Fitz shouted his last "All aboard!" Sam put on his driver's gloves and leaned his head far out the window, waiting for the all clear before blowing the whistle and throttling the train slowly forward.

To Drew, leaving the station from high atop the powerful engine was the consummate adventure. The sounds of the huge metal wheels on the tracks, the steam released from the brakes and the smells from the engine were intoxicating. As the driver, fireman and guard performed their jobs in sync, the passengers sat securely in their seats, trusting these railroaders would see them efficiently and safely to their destinations.

Sam turned to Drew and smiled. Her stomach did that annoying flip-flop again. He was so handsome in his striped coveralls with his cap perched on his head. He wore his engine driver's face, serious and focused now that they had left the station. He took out his pocket watch attached to its silver chain, a treasured gift from his father. "Right on time: 8:01!" Slipping the watch back into his pocket, Sam nodded to Drew, her cue to blow the whistle as they left the Swansea station to ride the 300 km of tracks east to London.

Sam's father would, as always, be waiting for them at the Paddington station in his big black coupe. As Sam finished his tasks, including the paperwork completed each time an engine driver completed a run, Drew went to gather her belongings. Not wanting to bother Fitz, who was busy with debarking passengers and unloading freight, she climbed the stairs of the brake van and secured her garment bag and case. She loved the small cabooses almost as much as she loved the huge train engines. Granda told her that during the first war he had lived for weeks at a time in the brake van of the troop train he ran, the last car of the train. He had put in a small wood stove for warmth and stoked it high when he needed to cook on the top of it in his single pan. He said that despite the brutal realities of wartime, living there was a great adventure. And there was solace in being alone, watching over his train.

Knowing she still had a little time before Sam was ready to leave, Drew sat down on the wooden bench of the brake van and looked out the window. Craning her neck, she could see almost to the engine. She liked watching the passengers being greeted by family and friends. Even in these hard post-war days, people found hope and joy in what they still had. And this was the first holiday without war in so many years. There was hope in that.

Sam finished his duties and together they found Douglas, Sam's father, waiting for them in the usual spot, leaning against his car parked just beyond the station's entrance. Seeing them both, he jumped forward, popped the boot and gave them both tight hugs, one that squeezed the breath out of Drew. She loved Mr. Provens and hugged him back as hard as she could.

"How was the trip? Did you get to ride up front, Drew?"

"She would have it no other way, Father. I had to hold tight to the throttle, knowing at any moment she may wrestle it away from me."

"That's the way, Drew. Fight for what you want and don't let anyone stop you, especially this fellow," said Mr. Provens, giving Drew a big smile while clapping Sam on the back. His joy at seeing them both radiated from his person. His aura was a bright rainbow of color and filled Drew with happiness.

After stowing their belongings in the boot, Drew tumbled into the back seat, the men in the front, and off they sped to Sam's family home. Father and son talked all the way to Hampstead Heath, as Drew watched out the window, noting again the bombed buildings and piles of rubble that she had seen from the engine's cab, which increased as they drove through the streets of London. Her happiness quickly evaporated into despair.

Douglas and Kathleen's home, Pine Grove Manor, stood on a grassy hill that backed up to an old pine forest just outside of the city. The house was a large two-story in the Georgian architectural style. It had been built by Sam's great-great-grandfather, who was also the founder of the banking firm now run by Mr. Provens. The estate, along with the banking dynasty, had been handed down from father to son. That is, until Sam, who had absolutely no aspirations to enter the financial world and as far as Drew could tell was never pressured by his parents to do so.

Kathleen Provens stood waiting for them on the circular drive as they drove up to the front of the stately home. Drew stepped from the car quickly, eager to hug Sam's mother and smell the delicious fragrance of her cologne, a blend of something both floral and spicy. It always reminded Drew of dessert, and it did so again today, her stomach reminding her they hadn't eaten since a light breakfast.

"Drew, oh, how wonderful to see you. Truly, you become lovelier every time you visit. Come into the house while these two take your bags up. I know you must be famished. Poppy has lunch ready. She won't tell me what it is, but says she made it especially for her favorite engine driver. . . . And I know she isn't talking about Sam," she added with a laugh. Arm in arm, Kathleen led Drew into the lovely home where delicious smells teased Drew's nose in excited anticipation of the meal ahead.

Seated at the large dining room table, which was covered by a white linen cloth and set with beautiful china in a room that could only be described as exquisite and warm, Drew felt as comfortable as she did in her own small cottage in Mumbles. After putting the food on the table, Poppy sat down on the other side of Drew and began passing dishes.

Poppy was a bona fide member of the Provens family and had been Sam's nanny. When he and his sister were too old for that role, she became both housekeeper and cook, sharing all the kitchen responsibilities with Mrs. Provens, a skilled cook herself.

"I expect to see your plate piled high, young lady, and more than once," said Poppy in her familiar Welsh accent. She was originally from Swansea and felt a strong connection to Drew just by right of heritage.

Taking each platter in turn, Drew filled her plate with a fillet of fresh fish, crisp browned potatoes, a generous portion of tomato aspic, and two slices of a crusty loaf of bread. Her bread plate already had a perfect round of butter on it, and she longed to slather each piece with the yellow gold and savor every bite. But she put her hands on her lap and waited until the others had served themselves. She marveled that with rationing still an ever-present part of all their lives, the Provens were able to lay such a generous table, noting that there was still enough aspic for another slice and hopefully more butter, should she need it.

Douglas rose from his chair and took the bottle of white wine from the glass bowl where it lay chilling, then filled each person's crystal glass with a bubbly liquid. Drew realized it was champagne, which she loved, and it would go wonderfully with the lunch choices. Standing at the head of the table, Mr. Provens lifted his glass and said, "To family and friends, Kathleen and I are so thankful you are here for the party. This makes the holidays even more special. Here's to you both."

They all raised their glasses and drank. As the bubbles tickled Drew's nose, as she had hoped, she felt her eyes welling with tears. Bubbles of hope and tears of gratitude. Blinking them back, Drew tucked into her food, laying as much butter on the bread as possible while still hoping to be polite. When she glanced up before taking that first bite, she saw Kathleen looking at her, a loving smile on her face as she winked at Drew.

Kathleen and Poppy refused Drew's help to clear the table but requested that she and Sam bundle up and walk to the forested area at the back of their property to cut some pine boughs. Kathleen needed at least fifteen long swags to complete her decorations for tomorrow's party. Sam and Drew quickly donned their coats and gloves and out into the cold they went, Sam carrying the saw his father provided.

"It's wonderful to be here, Sam. Your family is always so welcoming and kind. Thank you for inviting me to come up with you. I'm looking forward to the party."

"You know they love having you here, and I hope you know I do too." Sam stopped walking and turned to Drew. "I sometimes feel guilty that my life is so good and that I am so happy."

"You have absolutely nothing to feel guilty about. Be thankful all of your family survived the last years." Drew paused thoughtfully, then asked, "What is it about your life that makes you so happy?"

Sam pondered that as they continued towards the tall trees ahead. "Well, I have the job I always dreamt of, good people to work with, wonderful parents who are supportive, a great sister and now nephews, and, of course, the war is over and hopefully we can all get on with life. And I've been wanting to tell you, I have almost enough saved to get my own place. I've my eye on a cottage not far from your grandparents. It's bigger, though, three bedrooms and a larger kitchen and sitting room. Outbuildings too. Maybe you can look at it with me after Christmas."

Sam stopped and turned to look at Drew again. "And you, Drew, are you happy?"

"Well, if we're being honest, I have a job that is tolerable but in no way challenging or fulfilling, and the job I want will never be mine because I am a woman. I will never see my parents or brother again, never have nieces or nephews, and I have so many unanswered questions about the death of my family that I think it keeps me stuck in the present without a concrete plan for my future.

"Of course, Granda and Nonna are my family, and I love them with my whole heart, and certainly Serena is family as well. I know I am loved and love them all in return, but it will never be the whole family I could have had. And all that makes me feel sad and guilty, knowing I am not the only one carrying grief. Everyone has lost someone and so much. So, am I happy? Well, I guess I am restlessly contented and trying to figure out what's next."

Sam nodded in response to all Drew shared, his eyes to the ground as they turned and continued walking. "And what about us? I hope you know that I am someone you can count on, that I care about you."

It was Drew who stopped now. She looked up into Sam's eyes. "I know you do, and I care for you. You are my best friend, Sam, and I'm sorry that I am sometimes not the friend I need to be. I'm going to try and be better about that."

Sam laughed. "I never want you to be anything but what you are, which is wonderful. You're my best friend too, but I want you to know that I am hoping our friendship becomes more." Drew didn't respond so Sam continued, "Does that scare you when I say that? I don't want to risk our friendship by wanting something more if that's not on."

"For now, I think we are just where we need to be in this time of the world trying to right itself." Drew took his hand and held on tightly. When they reached the trees, she said, "Who knows what the new year will bring, but I am hoping for good things, and I know our friendship is one we can both count on. Let's enjoy this holiday time and not think too much about what's next."

As they stepped deep into the woods, Sam threw his arm round Drew's shoulder and said with great cheer, "I do know this Christmas will be better than any we have had in a long time, and there is no one I would rather spend it with than you and my family."

Some hours later, Drew found herself alone in the elegant bedroom that was designated as hers whenever she stayed with Sam's family. Her thoughts went to Charlotte and Eira, knowing they might be especially lonely this year, and adding to their grief, there were still no answers as to who killed the vicar and why.

Drew sighed. The clock on the dresser showed nearly eight o'clock. Time to put such dreary thoughts aside. She heard guests arriving for the party, being greeted by Mr. and Mrs. Provens. She couldn't pick out Sam's voice but knew he would be there beside his parents, welcoming friends into their home.

She had taken time earlier to carefully lay her beautiful velvet dress out across the wide bed. Her stockings, still wrapped in tissue, lay beside the dress and her new shoes sat neatly on the floor. As she did her hair and makeup at the vanity, she listened to the happy chatter of the people below.

Her heart fluttered when she heard Sam greet his sister and her husband. Her hands fell to her lap as she imagined having her own family and realized when she did that it was Sam she saw beside her, greeting family and friends at the cottage he was thinking of buying.

Drew sighed again, this time at her foolishness. She picked up the hairbrush and began piling her lush copper curls atop her head, attempting to place the pins and combs into her hair as Nonna had shown her. Looking into the mirror and turning her head side to side, she was happily surprised to see her efforts almost matched those of Nonna's. She lightly applied the face cream and added a dot of color to both her cheeks and lips. The mirror's reflection told her she looked her best and would do justice to the lovely dress.

As she slipped into the blue velvet, realizing she would need someone to do up the back, there was a knock at her door.

"Drew, may I come in?" It was Sam's sister, Claire, coming to say hello before the festivities began. Drew opened the door and Claire swept into the room.

"It's wonderful to see you, Claire," said Drew, welcoming the other woman's warm embrace. "And you are just the person I need to help me. Can you please button the back of my dress?"

"You look absolutely lovely, Drew. I have never seen you with your hair up, and it is very flattering. And this dress! Wherever did you find it in these days?"

"My godmother, Serena, made it for me, along with some other clothes I've brought. She was a seamstress much of her life and has kept the fabric hidden away in a cedar trunk. I feel like a princess."

"You certainly look the part. And I think your handsome prince, otherwise known as my little brother, is anxiously waiting for you downstairs," said Claire as she gently brushed the velvet of Drew's dress.

"I only need to put on my earrings. My granda gave them to me before I left," said Drew, placing the buds of sparkling blue sapphires onto her ears. "He isn't such a sentimental man, and I was so touched."

"Wait here and I'll go tell Sam you're ready. A princess should always make an entrance."

"A princess? Entrance? I'll probably fall headlong down the stairs," mused Drew to herself as she slid into her shoes and walked to the door, not surprised to find the butterflies alive and well in her stomach.

Taking several deep breaths, she walked to the head of the stairs and paused. Sure enough, there was Sam waiting at the bottom of the long staircase with a grand smile on his face and looking so handsome in his tuxedo. Who knew he even had one? Holding firmly to the banister, she started down the thickly carpeted stairs, returning Sam's smile as he held his hand out to her.

"You're the most beautiful aspiring railway engine driver I've ever seen, Drew Davies!"

"*Diolch*, Samuel Provens. And you certainly do justice to that tuxedo. I didn't see you bring a bag it would have fit into."

"I leave it here, along with a wardrobe full of other clothes I would never wear in Swansea."

Sam steered Drew into the salon, where they were met with the vision of a towering pine tree decorated with iridescent glass balls of jeweled colors reflecting the light from the many flickering candles placed all about the room. The sight took Drew's breath away, but before she could walk over to admire the elegant tree, Sam took her elbow and led her to where his parents were visiting with his sister, her husband, Matthew, and several friends.

Seeing them approach, Kathleen held out her hand to Drew, kissed her on the cheek, then introduced her to those she did not know. Having finished the introductions, Kathleen leaned over and whispered in Drew's ear, "You look exquisite. It makes my heart so happy that you are with us. Thank you for coming, dear."

"Thank you, Mrs. Provens. I truly feel as though I am in a fairy tale."

As more people approached Sam and his family, Drew slipped away to walk the ground floor, room by room. Small groups were gathered in each one, everyone holding a glass of champagne.

The air was filled with the energy of grateful celebration. Drew saw auras of white light round many of the guests, including Sam and his family. Smiling, she took her own glass of champagne from a butler's tray as she continued her walk about the house.

She noticed that the lovely dresses and gowns worn by the women were most likely not new but brought out and shaken off for tonight, waking memories of past Christmases and making promises that tonight was the beginning of better times. The same with the men's suits and tuxedos. Clothes that had hung in wardrobes through many years of war were now ready to be worn again to welcome revival. She raised her glass in a silent salute to them all.

As Drew moved slowly through each room, smiling and greeting people that spoke a greeting to her, she discovered that a Christmas tree graced each one, and every tree was decorated in a different theme. One was covered in bright silver and red ornaments, another with different shapes and sizes of icicles made of crystal amid shining balls of blue glass. These ornaments must hold memories of Christmases celebrated in this grand home by many past generations of Provenses. Nothing about the décor was ostentatious but instead subtle, even sparse, allowing the good bones of the lovely house to reflect all that was precious to this wonderful family.

In another room, a space she realized was meant as a playroom with its rocking horse and small table and chairs topped with books and blocks, there was a tree decorated with ornaments that could only have been made by children. Most of them looked many years old. Drew knew these were cherished keepsakes. Stepping closer to the tree, she found the ornaments were made of thin wood or cardboard in the shapes of snowflakes and snowmen, silver stars, and green holly, the colors faded with time. And a host of them were in the shapes of trains—train engines, train cars and brake vans. She knew immediately that these were made by Sam.

A model train moved round and round on tracks laid at the bottom of this charming children's tree. This, too, must be Sam's. As Drew carefully touched each ornament, Sam walked up to her side.

"As you can see, my mother keeps everything from when we were young. I don't know whether to be grateful or embarrassed."

"This is my favorite tree of all the lovely ones in your family's home, Sam." Drew looked around her. "And this is my favorite room. I could stay here all evening looking through the books and stacking the blocks. What a wonderful space. You and Claire must have spent such fun times here."

"We did, and now my nephews will do the same. There is something to be said for family traditions, and no one does them better than Mother. I hope someday when I visit with my own children they'll play here as well."

"I am sure they will. And I would have a room just like this one in my own home, for my own children."

"Well, on that we can agree. A house large enough for a children's playroom."

They looked at each other with smiles of possibility. Finally, Drew looked down at the table and picked up one of the books, opening its cover—a book all about trains.

"That book was my favorite. I took it to bed with me every night."

It always amazed Drew that from such a young age Sam, like herself, was fascinated with trains. It also surprised her that Sam's parents seemed to readily accept that, after completing his time at university studying engineering, he enlisted in the army and served two years in the British Railway Battalion. At the end of the war, Howard, on the recommendation from a military comrade, secured Sam a position as an engine driver working out of the Swansea station.

As Drew glanced again at the miniature train winding its way round the decorated tree, she knew Sam's wishes, at least regarding his career, had come true for him. She wondered if that same wish would ever become a reality for her. Shaking off the melancholy of her dreams, she knew she could wish all she wanted, but the reality was that the world, at least in Britain, was far from accepting women into the business of railroading.

CHAPTER 19

THE MAN IN THE BOWLER HAT – SATURDAY, 7 DECEMBER

When Drew and Sam left the children's playroom and entered the large parlor, she was startled as she caught sight of one of the guests. It was Bowler Hat. Even without the black hat perched atop his head, she was positive it was the same man that approached her at the train station and had been lurking round the vicarage. What on earth was he doing here?

"Sam, do you know who that man is standing over by the window, the one balding on top?"

"That's Mr. William Sussex, the bank's solicitor. He and father have known each other for years. Mr. Sussex has become a friend of the family, though all I ever hear him and father talk about is bank business and some issue they were involved in with the government during the war. Father is always saying, 'Wars run on money and banks manage and move it.' Father has mentioned on many occasions that he trusts Mr. Sussex implicitly, and should I ever have an occasion to need good financial counsel, he should be the person I go to."

"It's curious that I see Mr. Sussex in Mumbles frequently. Not as much lately but definitely over the last year. He rode the train regularly from Swansea to

London, and he recently asked me about Vesuvi, did I know what happened to the vicar's cat. Now why in the world would he be interested?"

Sam put his hand to the small of Drew's back, saying, "Let's walk over, and I'll have father introduce you, and maybe you can find out."

The last time Drew saw Mr. Sussex was in her ticket queue when he asked rudely and without preamble if she knew the whereabouts of the cat. At that time, he seemed a man on a mission, was curt, and didn't much appreciate Drew's equally curt and noncommittal reply regarding Vesuvi.

Coming alongside his father, Sam asked, "Father, would you introduce Drew to Mr. Sussex? It seems they have seen each other in Mumbles."

"Of course. Come this way." Douglas led Drew and Sam across the room to where the man stood talking with two other gentlemen. "Pardon me, William, I'd like you to meet Miss Drew Davies. Drew is a friend of Sam's, and she has also become a friend of Kathleen and myself. We are delighted she could join us this weekend."

Mr. Sussex, to Drew's amazement, smiled and then paused slightly before holding out his hand. "Hello again, Miss Davies. I must apologize for my rude behavior at the railway station last month. It had been a harrowing day, and I had hoped to gather much needed information before I boarded the train back to London. Unfortunately, I didn't find what I was looking for and unfairly took my frustration out on you by asking a rather random question."

Drew returned his smile and realized her feelings towards this man were still tinged with caution. Should she ask why he was so curious about a cat?

Before she could ask, Claire appeared at her side, linking her arm through Drew's and giving her cheek a kiss. "I feel as if we are in a dream. It is hard to believe the war is over, and we are here, all together at Christmas, safe once again with all the ones we love. I cannot tell you how wonderful it is to have you here, Drew."

"I always love visiting your parents' home, but you are right, tonight is wonderful, magical really. And the Christmas trees in each of the rooms are marvelous. I especially love the one in the children's room with all of Sam's and your homemade decorations."

Mr. Sussex held up a finger, bowing his head slightly, and said, "You will please excuse me now. Lovely to see you again, Miss Davies." He then turned and walked through the room to pick up conversation with a group standing by the large Christmas tree.

Drew could not take her eyes off him, but Claire didn't seem to notice and kept right on talking as if Sussex had never even been there. "And this is the first year Benji will be old enough to make his first ornament for the tree! It will only be squiggles of color, of course, but will become my very favorite of all time."

All smiles, Drew said, "I do hope to see baby Samuel before we go back. How does Benji like having a little brother?"

"They seem to adore one another. If they get along half as well when they are eight and ten as they do now, it will be smooth sailing for all of us. And we will be here with the boys tomorrow for an early breakfast before you and Sam leave."

As Claire was speaking, Drew kept half an eye on Bowler Hat, for that is how she knew she would always think of Mr. Sussex. He had wandered away into another room, and when Claire went to mingle with other guests, Drew made a beeline to find him.

She found the solicitor in the library, looking out one of the windows to the manicured lawn and gardens. The room was appointed with beautiful dark wood shelves along three sides, ceiling to floor, and filled with leather-bound books. Set about the room were several small side tables next to large upholstered chairs in a tapestried fabric of maroon and dark blue. An enormous oriental carpet covered most of the wood floor and thick drapes of dark blue velvet hung from the windows, pulled back at the sides by ornate silver tiebacks. Drew wished she could have closed the door and spent days in there just perusing all the tomes and reading from dawn to dark.

She knocked quietly on the door jamb and Mr. Sussex turned. "Ah, Miss Davies. I thought you might come looking for me. I sense we have some unfinished business. Douglas told me you were the one that found Alred Hughes's body and may have questions regarding the murder, and as I am sure you deduced from my questions about his cat, I have some interest in that regard as well."

Drew nodded and entered the softly lit room, so conducive for such a serious conversation. The man sat down on a brown leather couch facing the window and, with a motion of his hand, invited Drew to do the same.

"I need you to know, Miss Davies, that I am working with the police in Wales, in addition to the government, in connection with the murder of Vicar Hughes. If you need that substantiated, you have but to ask the Swansea authorities. On second thought, however, they probably won't confirm my involvement, as they are a very tight-lipped lot regarding this whole affair and who has jurisdiction in the ongoing investigation of the murder."

Drew took a seat before saying, "That goes some way in explaining why you were interested in the vicar's cat. I think I have some idea as to why but am not sure what I can ask."

"The vicar is dead and the war is over, so yes, I can probably answer some of your questions. How much do you actually know about Alred Hughes?"

Drew took several moments before she replied, studying this man before her. Could she trust him? She saw his aura was a hazy brown and hard to read, but his countenance was forthcoming, and because she knew Sam's father held Mr. Sussex in high esteem and considered him a friend, she decided to share her impressions.

"I know that he was murdered, that he was involved in what may have been espionage of some sort, and that I rescued his cat, which is now mine. The cat, Vesuvi, came to me wearing a large bell round his neck containing two small keys. I think the keys may lead to finding information regarding his work with the government as well as something of substance regarding his family. Is there any truth to my deductions, Mr. Sussex?"

"You say you cleaned the vicar's house, and I know you work at the railway station with your grandfather, Howard Davies. So how is it that you have any interest in the vicar's personal affairs at all, much less his murder?"

"My grandfather and I returned to the vicarage once I had packed up all his belongings, as the church requested. I had found it strange during my times there cleaning that there was no staircase, even though I knew there must be least one room above. I assume you know that too."

"Yes, I am well aware of that upper-floor room."

"Well, I found the ladder of sorts in the kitchen pantry. I showed Granda, and we found a large room equipped with what looks like a military radio transmitter, teletype machine, typewriter, telescope, and a various assortment of maps, journals and ledgers, all indicating movements of vessels and planes. It was obvious that the vicar was leading a double life, clergyman to some and man of complicity to others. And because of your many trips to Mumbles and asking about the cat, I now assume you were there to meet with the vicar, that you were involved in whatever it was he was doing for the government."

"Very capable sleuthing on your and your grandfather's part. Was he a military man himself?"

"Yes, he served in both wars, in the railway military battalion. I suspect he did some of what you call 'sleuthing' as well. So, of course, we are both curious as to what actually happened to the vicar, and is his murder in any way connected with what we found in the upper room, and is it tied to his work during the war."

"Well, I can tell you that his work with the war department spanned the duration of this last war and ended on the day of his murder. However, there are loose ends in the form of documents he was to pass on to me, but of course, I never received them after his death. You see, my trips to Mumbles were to meet with Alred, and he would give me what information he had gathered about enemy ship and troop movements along the coast. I in turn passed on any further instructions from those he took his orders from. I was merely the go-between. I carried information back and forth, but I never knew what the information was."

Drew listened intently and with renewed skepticism, keeping silent in hopes he would continue. He picked up his glass of champagne, drained it down as though incredibly thirsty, and began again.

"We had an arrangement in place, Alred and myself, that if he was ever unable to meet me and had important information I needed to get back to

London, he would ring my office phone once and hang up. He would do this three times, and I would know then to go to Mumbles, get the key from the cat's bell and retrieve the documents from a locker in the railway station. Obviously, I do not have that key. But now that you are here, Miss Davies, and know the story, I am hoping that I can finalize the government's business with Hughes."

Drew rose and went to stand by the window, staring out into the dark night, giving herself some moments to think about all that was said. "And what is it that you think I can help you with, Mr. Sussex?"

"You do understand that I need the locker opened and must take possession of the documents inside."

Drew turned to face him. "Surely you could not have been waiting to just randomly make my acquaintance at a social gathering to ask about the key. If you needed access to the locker at the station, why haven't you gone to the local police or to my grandfather? He is the station master and would have the authority to open the locker, that is, if he knew it was at the bequest of the government."

"All true, Miss Davies, all true. But people above me, remember I am but the liaison, those above me wanted to wait until the murder investigation was further along. The government wanted to stay far from any association of murder. According to the police, and what they have determined, it isn't believed that his murder was in any way associated with his work with the war department. Now that that appears clear, this Monday I was to go to Mumbles, request that the locker be opened and take back to London whatever documents it contained. At least, those associated with his work with the military."

"We have the locker key, Mr. Sussex. As you knew, it was in the cat's bell. The number is ground off and not legible, but I did recognize it as a locker key from the station. It will be easy enough to determine which locker the vicar rented from the records kept in the office.

"I have one final question. Obviously, you met with Alred Hughes at the vicarage. Was his sister ever there when you and he were talking?"

"Yes. I met him at the vicarage on several occasions, and his sister, I believe her name is Eira, was there at least two of those times. I got the impression that she assisted him in some way in his work for the government. Alred spoke freely when she was there about what he had observed and communicated. But both times when she was present, she attempted to interject something into Alred's comments, and both times he stopped her immediately with a harsh reprimand for interrupting him. And in both instances, she appeared very upset by her brother's harsh chastisements and quickly left the room. I remember thinking it must have been very embarrassing for her."

"Did they seem generally at odds with one another when you were present?"

"Well, only seeing them together twice, it is hard to say, but it was obvious they were not kindly disposed to each other when I was with them. They always appeared nervous, ready to jump at any moment. Neither were friendly to me by any means. I think they were very similar in their temperaments. Maybe that is why, even though they didn't appear to like one another's company, they got the business done."

Sussex rose, preparing to leave, but stopped short. "I understand that Alred Hughes's daughter, Charlotte Parkinson Hughes, has an appointment with the bank on Monday, as she has secured her father's will. And Miss Parkinson Hughes will also have the key to a safe deposit box registered in her name. I will be at the bank with Charlotte and Mr. Provens when she takes possession of the box's contents."

Drew had an idea. "Why don't you plan on traveling to Swansea on the morning train this Tuesday. Both my granda and I will be at the station working as usual. I will tell my grandfather about all of this before your arrival. You can talk with him further about the locker's contents. I assume you will bring documentation showing you are authorized by the government and the police to take any papers that indicate they belong to the government."

He merely nodded his head while giving Drew a dark look. He was obviously not relishing such a conversation with this meddling young woman. "Let's say, Miss Davies, I will arrive on the 12:10 from London. I look forward to speaking about this matter with Station Master Davies and Chief Inspector Lewis." Without another look or word, Bowler Hat turned and left the room.

Drew was trembling slightly with a strange energy pulsing though her body. She felt as though she had watched the entire conversation from outside herself. Who in the world was this confident young woman who had spoken so succinctly, held herself so straight, and was not in the least intimidated by the solicitor, Mr. Sussex? She knew that was the most adult conversation of her life and one she enjoyed more than any before it. And the conversation had made her ravenous. She would find Sam and then find food.

CHAPTER 20

AN ACCOUNTING –
SUNDAY, 8 DECEMBER

T he following day, Drew woke early and lay in the large bed thinking over all that had occurred at the party. The memories were pleasant and brought smiles until her conversation with Mr. Sussex made its way into her thoughts. And now, rather than recalling the kind people she met, dancing with Sam as the string quartet played, the glowing candles placed about the beautiful house, the charming decorated trees, and the delicious food served throughout the evening, all Drew could focus on was her conversation with Bowler Hat.

She had rung Granda late last night after the party, before she settled into bed, recounting the conversation with Mr. Sussex and that the man planned to be at the station on Tuesday to take possession of any government papers in locker #17. She also shared that Mr. Provens, having been brought up to date on finding the vicar's will and what it stipulated, left a message with Charlotte at the B and B, arranging to meet him at the bank on Monday, where she would be assisted in opening the safe deposit box and retrieving whatever waited for her there. Drew asked Granda to take the safe deposit box key from her satchel and give it to Charlotte before she left for London.

She would ring Charlotte early enough this Sunday morning, but not so early that she would provoke the wrath of the landlady, telling her to be sure she connected with Granda to get the key and to be on that morning train. She would meet Charlotte at the station, and they would drive directly to the bank.

With that plan settled, knowing it was far too early to tramp downstairs to ring Charlotte or for several cups of coffee, Drew settled back under the quilts, hoping to fall back asleep.

Sunday seemed to go on forever. Drew kept herself busy helping Poppy prepare lunch, as Claire had called to say she would be bringing Benji and baby Sammy over about noon. Although it was wonderful to see the boys, Drew's mind was on tomorrow's events at the bank. She was thankful that Charlotte was resourceful and composed. Drew was eager to see her and reassure herself that, indeed, the woman was taking this all in stride.

Sam knew and understood Drew's restless anxiety, and as he played with his nephews and visited with his sister, he occasionally glanced Drew's way, gently trying to distract her from worrying. He hoped that once Charlotte arrived at Paddington, and they drove her to the bank, all would be well.

Monday morning, Sam and Drew took his father's car and met Charlotte's train just as it was pulling into the station. As soon as Charlotte alighted from the train, any concerns Drew had regarding her state of mind were put to rest. The woman wore her all-business skirt and matching jacket, coat, and gloves. Her head was held high, her posture erect, with her purse firmly in the crook of her arm. And Drew knew the safe deposit key was tucked safely inside the handbag. Charlotte was a capable woman on a serious mission, and her deep red aura reflected as much. The two women were more than glad to see each other and immediately began conversing as Sam led the way to the car.

Sam found a place to park and escorted Drew and Charlotte through the bank's cavernous main lobby. Drew was not surprised to see Sam greeted by employees who seemed genuinely happy to see him, and shortly after, his father, along with Mr. Sussex, appeared. Mr. Provens seemed very proud to have his son once again in the bank, a place and its people obviously very familiar to him.

"I understand you knew my father well?" asked Charlotte shortly after being introduced to Mr. Sussex, homing right in on the matter at hand. Mr. Provens and Sam had remained in the lobby as Charlotte and Drew were led away by Sussex, presumably towards the bank's large vault.

"I knew Alred for many years," Bowler Hat said stoically as he led the way down one of the banks many halls, never looking round when answering Charlotte.

"You were a friend then?" tried Charlotte again.

"No, I was never his friend. I was a liaison between Alred and the government and, therefore, the bank. But I was never his friend."

"I have a question, Mr. Sussex. You witnessed Mr. Hughes's will, leaving this money to Charlotte. Knowing as you did of the will's existence and its contents, why did you never come forward after his death and at least speak to the authorities?" asked Drew.

"The last time I saw him was at the vicarage, when I went to tell him that now that the war was over, his services to the government were no longer needed, and I delivered his final payment. He was to ring me when he had his final documents completed, and we would meet in the railway station and remove the last of the papers from the locker, which he felt was the safest place to keep them. Those are the papers I will secure from that locker when we meet tomorrow.

"As I was about to leave his house that last time, he produced some other papers, a new will, he said. He knew I was a solicitor and could witness and sign the document.

"It wasn't any concern of mine what the will said or didn't say. I briefly looked it over, saw it was all in order and placed my signature where it was required. After I left that day, I never saw the man again."

Drew persisted. "You still haven't answered my question. Why didn't you come forward after the murder and tell the police you had signed a new will that he had written. Did you not think it might have had something to do with his death?"

Bowler Hat stopped abruptly and turned round to face the women. "I've already told you that his personal affairs were none of my concern. I didn't know who Charlotte was, had no idea of his history, and I didn't care. Truthfully, I just wanted to be done with him and leave."

"I think the authorities would have cared that you knew about the will, and I'm sure you know that. Obviously, she was his daughter and closest next of kin." Drew was close to losing patience with Bowler Hat.

They stopped in front of a set of tall wooden double doors. He produced a key, placed it in the lock and said, "Well, it's over now. You'll soon have what you came for, and then, after tomorrow, this affair will be ended, at least as far as it concerns me and this bank."

He motioned to a man sitting at a nearby desk, turned the key in the lock and walked away from them. The man summoned walked up to them, saying, "Follow me and please have your key ready."

Before stepping through the doors, Drew turned round to see Bowler Hat standing some ways off, watching them. The man was of two faces. One polite and almost gracious when in the company of men and women of position and authority, especially when he perceived the men in the group to be powerful. And the second face obtuse and rude when it suited him, especially when his intentions were questioned, and by a woman, at that.

She understood now that their conversation the night of the party was cordial only because he wanted information from her. She knew the conversation at the bank today would have gone much differently had Mr. Provens remained with them. Drew was thankful they had walked alone with him through the halls of the bank, seeing this chameleon for what he was. Surely the authorities would be interested in talking to William Sussex, Esq. of the Bowler Hat. But then again, perhaps the authorities had been in contact with the man since the vicar was murdered.

Drew suspected they would never know exactly what the vicar had been involved in, as no one was meant to know. But she was reassured knowing her first impressions had been correct: Sussex was not someone to be trusted. As she glanced back once more before going through the doors with Charlotte, the man's aura was dark, almost as dark as the look of fury on his face. Was that the face of a murderer?

Drew and Sam took the late afternoon train home, riding with the other passengers rather than in the engine. Drew was quiet, thinking over all that Mr. Sussex said and the way he behaved. She didn't trust him and felt that he was never really telling the truth, twisting and turning what he said depending on who he was addressing.

• • • •

"Granda, can we sit for a bit, a cup of tea maybe?" It was ten p.m. and Nonna had retired to their room, and it seemed a good time to talk to Granda about what she experienced in London.

"I'll put the kettle on and you get the cups. Then you tell me all of what's on your mind."

They seated themselves at the table, and Vesuvi promptly seated himself on Drew's lap as she gathered her thoughts.

"I saw quite a bit of Mr. Sussex over the time we were in London. Sam told me he was the bank's solicitor and over the years had become a family friend. He was at the party at Sam's parents', and we had an interesting conversation in their library. He was cordial enough, and I think he wanted to appear forthcoming, answering my questions about the vicar and making sure I understood he was merely a liaison between Vicar Hughes and the government.

"But then, the following day, when Charlotte and I met him at the bank to open her security box, he was less than cordial, especially to Charlotte. Belligerent, really. He seemed quite a different person from the other night. I believe him to be a man of secrets and a dual personality. Do you think he knows more about what happened to the vicar than he is saying?"

Granda stared off in thought and took a long drink of his tea before looking again at Drew. "You know, the police are not saying much about Alred's murder, and I find that unusual. It leads me to think that the government is involved in some way, maybe telling the local authorities to keep a distance until they do their own investigation."

"What we found in the upstairs room, could whatever Alred was doing for Britain and maybe also for Germany be the reason he was killed?"

"What I suspect is that Alred was making money from both sides. Mumbles Hill, Lighthouse Island, and all along the coastline to Swansea was well fortified with artillery installations and lookouts. Our military did not need Alred's information to monitor ship movements. However, the Germans would have paid nicely for his information about our own military activity along the coastline. As we first suspected, he could have been spying on us and then communicating the information to the Germans."

"So, he was a German spy? That is despicable!"

"Not necessarily. He could have been working with our government and feeding the German's false information. I think that is the more likely scenario. Again, he was making money from both sides. What we don't know is if the Germans found out and had him murdered or if our government came to distrust him and they killed him."

"That sounds like something right out of one of my books. While I find it all hard to believe, Granda, we do know the teletype and radio we found in the upstairs room were German, and we do know he was transmitting information. Also, he was giving information to our government via Mr. Sussex."

Howard, his cup now empty, folded his hands on the table, saying, "There is much espionage and subterfuge during war that goes on off the battlefields. If this is what Alred was involved in, working for our government via Mr. Sussex, then he would have certainly helped the war effort on our account."

Drew sighed. "Do you think we will ever know if any of that is true? Will it ever come out? And what about finding the vicar's murderer? If it was us or the Germans, how will it ever be resolved?"

"If his murder was an act of war, so to speak, the authorities will say that the murderer was never found, and the case will go unsolved and after a time be closed. Again, our own police may be told to tread lightly and officially conclude that the murder is unsolved and that is the end of it."

"But, of course, maybe neither side killed him but someone else altogether and just conveniently rid two governments of his presence."

"Ie, Drew Girl. This is merely a supposition on my part, as I have no facts to support any of my suspicions. And yes, the killer may have had nothing at all to do with wartime activities and may be a civilian."

"I don't think the government would have ransacked our home in search of the keys in Vesuvi's collar. And I would think our constables would still be looking for that person."

"And hopefully they are, Drew, but when I inquire, they merely say they have no suspects as yet. But it will be wise to keep a sharp eye for anything suspicious that has to do with the break-in here. And I agree that Mr. Sussex is a man of many faces.

"Chief Inspector Lewis called to let me know they will be coming to the station tomorrow and will be there with Mr. Sussex when we open the locker. And there they will find what they are looking for: papers left for Sussex in a manila envelope. I left it where it lay and carefully lifted out a smaller white envelope, again addressed to Charlotte. She and I had spoken Sunday afternoon, and I met her at the B and B. She opened the envelope and there it was, just the key, no note. She clutched it in her fist and said she would be at the station early to catch the train. She is a strong woman, and at least she has some small act of recompense from her father."

Drew yawned, rose, and rinsed her cup at the sink. She walked over to Granda and gave him a hug and a kiss on top of his head. "Yes. Charlotte does have some closure. Now, if she knew who killed her father, that would go a good distance to finishing this all up. And the break-in . . . I want to know, Granda."

Drew yawned wide again. "I am so happy to be sleeping tonight in my own bed, in my own room, in our own home. Good night, Granda. It was good to talk and gives us much to think about. I hope we both have a good sleep and no dreams of spying."

CHAPTER 21

CELEBRATIONS – TUESDAY, 10 DECEMBER

It seemed rather foolish that Drew felt nervous in her own home, especially when those coming this evening were people she wanted with her to celebrate her twenty-first birthday. Rather than feeling anxious, she should have been looking forward to her party. She wondered what was in store for the evening. She also needed to remember to ask Serena for a favor.

At 5:45 p.m., she was dressed and waiting in the kitchen for the first of her guests to arrive. This was more than a birthday dinner for her, as she had invited Charlotte and wanted her to feel welcome and included by her family.

As expected, Sam was the first to arrive. Besides Charlotte, he was the timeliest person she knew, and though people said it was because he worked for the railway and had to keep strict timetables, she knew it was also in his nature. He said if he was on time, it always felt late. Sam always enjoyed a social gathering, and she knew he especially loved coming to dinner with her family, so different from the more formal dinners at his parents' home.

Drew opened the door and was greeted with, "Happy Birthday, Miss Davies, and don't you look lovely this evening. I almost didn't recognize you."

"Are you saying, Mr. Provens, that my work attire is less than attractive?"

"*Na*," Sam responded, smiling his big, beautiful smile that always caught at her heart. "What you wear to work is good for the job, but I think I prefer what you wear to parties." He crossed the threshold and took her into his arms, kissing her on the cheek.

Drew returned the embrace, and when they parted, she glanced down at her gray wool trousers topped by a matching wool jumper. To her, the clothes were nothing that special, and the jumper was terribly scratchy. She preferred comfortable over dressy any day. But she did admit that when she dressed for special occasions, she felt attractive and quite grown up. And of course, turning twenty-one did qualify her as a fully fledged adult. She was glad Sam liked what she had chosen for this night's dinner.

"And you smell lovely," he added, as Drew returned his smile.

Seeing movement through the window, Drew stepped around him to open the door and found Serena standing there, shivering from the cold. She quickly stepped inside the kitchen, handing Drew two loaves of still-warm bread wrapped in tea towels as she swept past her.

"I do hope your granda keeps the fire blazing all evening. My feet and fingers are frozen, even with such a short walk from home."

"Granda piled on the wood, knowing you would say those exact words." Drew was always thankful that their property had two acres of forested land that provided an ample supply of wood. She so disliked using coal, and since it was still in short supply, it could go to others that needed it.

Serena hugged both Drew and Sam before pulling a linen-wrapped package from inside her coat and laying it on the edge of the table. She moved quickly to the fire as Naomi and Howard came into the kitchen from their room.

Howard and Naomi greeted their dear friend. "This inferno of a room warm enough for you, Serena?" asked Howard.

"Just be sure you keep it this way all evening, or you'll hear this old Italian woman complaining."

"Not on Drew's birthday, you wouldn't. Sam, if the fire gets low, can you to keep it to roaring?" said Howard as he shook Sam's hand. Naomi gave the young man a hug.

"Of course, Mr. Davies, no worries there."

"And this will warm you from the inside, Serena." Howard poured her a glass of rich red wine, the firelight reflected in the beautiful crystal glass, setting the wine aglow. He went on to fill and pass a glass to each guest, the new wine goblets replacing what had been shattered in the break-in.

He had brought eight glasses home last week, presenting them lovingly to Naomi. Each was wrapped in yellowed paper and layered in an old wooden box. When Naomi asked wherever did he find them, he said only that he acquired them through an old acquaintance he had met up with—someone he knew in France during the war. The gentleman, Henri Reichenbach, was a merchant who bought and sold fine pieces from estate sales in both France and England.

Nonna stood at the cooker and lifted the lid from a simmering pot of rich Bolognese, Drew's favorite dish, giving it a slow stir with her large wooden spoon. "I'll get that," she said, responding to the knock at the door.

"Charlotte! We are so happy that you are here. Come in, come in," welcomed Naomi.

Charlotte stood still on the wide step, making no move to enter.

Seeing the woman's hesitation, Drew hurried to the door and reached a hand out to her. "How wonderful to see you. Please, come in and get warm."

Charlotte relaxed and smiled and followed Drew to the hearth, where she stood in front of the fire beside Serena. Serena had finally warmed up enough to relinquish her coat, and Naomi took both hers and Charlotte's into the sitting room.

"Let me introduce everyone again," said Drew, "and I say 'again,' Charlotte, as you met most of us at the funeral."

Charlotte nodded politely as she greeted each person in turn. Serena, still standing beside Charlotte, gently laid a hand to the other women's arm and said quietly, "I am very sorry for your loss and the unsettling circumstances."

"Thank you. Yes, it has been rather surreal and continues to be unsettling with no news of who murdered my father."

Hearing these last words of Charlotte's, Howard said, "Murder is always unsettling and an especially terrible way to lose a relative. The police are continuing their investigation, and last I was told, no suspects have been identified and they have no credible leads." Charlotte merely nodded, looking as though she doubted any news would ever be forthcoming.

Nonna carried the heavy red pot from the cooker and set it atop the folded tea towel in the center of the table, then returned with a large platter of fresh pasta and a plate of asparagus from the canned goods in the cellar. "Let's sit now and put all thoughts of unpleasantness aside as we celebrate the life of our Drew."

"Yes, it's a birthday celebration," said Sam, pulling Drew's chair out for her on the side of the table opposite the fire.

As if on cue, Vesuvi jumped onto Drew's lap. She knew Granda would rather not have him at the table but also knew that if she didn't meet his eye, he would ignore such behavior on her birthday. Obviously, Vesuvi knew this as well and settled in comfortably. This left the two places in front of the hearth for Serena and Charlotte, where their backs would be kept warm throughout dinner.

"Sit across from me, Charlotte. I want to know all you have been up to since I last saw you," said Drew.

Sam quickly moved to the other side of the table and drew out Charlotte's chair and then Serena's.

Before Charlotte could answer, Serena sprang from the table. "I almost forgot the bread!" She hurried to the counter, unwrapped one of the loaves, quickly sliced it, then placed it on an oval platter and passed it round the table.

Charlotte watched Serena's keen efficiency and waited for her to take her seat before answering Drew. "There isn't much to tell, actually. Although, I have discovered the benefits of walking long distances, which has been good for my mind, not to mention my body, and I continue to spend some hours each day at the library. Your village is lovely and the people are most friendly. It is surprising, however, to see so much destruction. I don't think I realized how much damage the Germans did even here in such a quiet place relatively far from London. Were the railway tracks damaged severely enough to cause problems with the rail service, Mr. Davies?"

"The tracks are not as damaged as the rail companies themselves. There will be much reorganizing and refurbishing in the coming years and most likely a restructuring of the rail companies. I am choosing to think of the changes as necessary post-war reconstruction, which will, in the end, be beneficial to both the companies and the public. And please, call me Howard." He smiled and topped off everyone's glass. The table was quiet for several minutes as they tucked into Nonna's food.

Charlotte had been doubtful as to whether she would accept Drew's invitation, but now, looking round the table and feeling more comfortable, she thought should the right moment present itself she might share her news with them all. Until yesterday, she had given little thought to the future, other than reluctantly returning to her long-familiar surroundings in London. She had believed that returning to the depressingly familiar, her unrewarding university position and a house devoid of any happy memories, had been her only option. But after this time in Mumbles, going back to a future as lonely as the past seemed untenable. Would remaining here in the hopes of finding answers to who killed her father be a reasonable thing to do or just an excuse not to return to her empty life alone? But yesterday presented another option, a future filled with a new perspective and new possibilities.

Sam could not have been happier to be in this place, sitting beside Drew surrounded by her loving family. He could see himself often at this table, with Drew always next to him, their own cottage not far away.

Serena was curious about Charlotte. She knew Drew had befriended the woman, was helping her in trying to find answers to her father's death and the will that was found. She saw that the energy of Charlotte's aura was much calmer than at the funeral. But, of course, it would be. She wondered how much longer Charlotte would be here before having to return to London and resuming what sounded like a rather listless existence. However, she appeared content sitting at this table with the family, and Serena was happy for her.

Howard and Naomi had marveled this morning that Drew, their own Drew Girl, was turning twenty-one. They knew that one day she would leave their home, and it was almost too much to think about. But Howard reminded Naomi that, most likely, Drew would never travel far from Mumbles, the place she loved, and he hoped she would stay close enough to work at the station. Now, giving each other occasional knowing glances, both felt the evening was going well. They knew, apart from Drew's kindness, why Charlotte had been invited and were wondering if Drew and Charlotte would update everyone on their discoveries.

Conversations were quieting as everyone finished their meal. Charlotte set her knife and fork along her empty plate and took a deep breath. She looked round the table, hoping to catch the eyes of each person before beginning. "I want to thank you all for including me on this evening of Drew's birthday, truly a special occasion. Naomi, your food is some of the best I have eaten, by far the finest Italian food I have had. And thank you, Serena, for the bread, the sustenance of life, they say. Drew, you have shown me great kindness since you found me on my father's doorstep, and again, I thank you for that. I am finding that with the passing of days I am feeling reluctant to return to London.

"There is a peace here that I have never experienced in my life. I admit that while each day I hope to hear news regarding my father's death, at least I have found out, with the help of Drew and Howard, more about my father than I could have hoped and that he truly did remember me. Now, I can begin to let the past go and find my own peace.

"Perhaps Drew shared with you that my father's will was found, and he did indeed leave me what he felt was some atonement for his dismissal of me and Mother. It amounts to £30,000, quite a tidy sum." Looking to Drew, Charlotte sat a little straighter in her chair and went on. "I'd like you all to know that I have made some decisions and would like to share them, if that is not disruptive to the festivities, Drew."

"Please, Charlotte, you have me on the edge of my seat. When I saw your face at the door, I knew you had news so, please, share with us."

Granda glanced at Drew, giving her a slow nod and a slight smile.

"Well, so much has happened since father's will was found and the money came into my possession. At least having that settled is some relief, but even more exciting is that I have decided to retire from my position at university in London and move my residence to Mumbles."

Around the table, encouraging words and curious looks passed between them all.

"And how did you come to that decision, Charlotte?" asked Howard.

"Well, I mentioned to Lillian Powell at the library—you know her, Drew, the head librarian—that after spending time here, I realized I truly wanted to live in a place such as Mumbles but didn't know if there were any jobs for which I might be qualified outside of teaching. She told me that she was just about to post the opening for an assistant librarian, as the woman currently in that position had left to have a baby and remain home with her family."

"That is wonderful news, Charlotte," said Howard. "When are you thinking about making all these changes?"

Charlotte seemed hardly able to contain her enthusiasm as she replied, "Very soon, Mr. Davies—I mean, Howard. Yesterday, I rang an estate agent in London, and my home will be up for sale in three days. I then notified the university, letting them know I was retiring and would not be returning for the new term. I will meet with them next week as well as with the estate agent and sign all the necessary papers on both counts."

Charlotte was breathless after conveying all her news as she glanced hopefully from person to person, looking for confirmation that she was absolutely making the right decisions.

Drew reached across the table for Charlotte's hands and held them in her own. "I for one am incredibly excited for you, Charlotte! And working at the library with Lillian could not be more perfect for you. The two of you appear to have become fast friends already."

"We certainly have, and until I can find my own small place to live, she has offered me a room in her home. Of course, I will pay her rent, and of course, we both hope it works out amicably. It may be challenging to work together all day and then return to the same living space in the evenings, but she and I have talked and talked about it, and she seems as excited as I am.

"Oh dear, I am taking up so much time with my news. I do apologize and thank you so much for your support. It feels grand to have people to talk to about such a drastic change of circumstances."

Nonna began gathering up the dishes. "Well, it isn't often that we have such interesting and happy news. I think I can say we are all very happy for you Charlotte and will enjoy having you as part of our community. And I hope you grace us with your presence at many dinners to come."

"The money your father left you should go a long way in helping you secure a home here," said Howard, taking spoons and small bowls from Naomi and placing them on the table.

"Yes, yes, it is a considerable amount of money, and after some thought and wanting a clear conscience, I have passed all but £5,000 on to Eira. I am sure she was expecting her brother to leave her something,, rather than bequeath everything he had to a bastard daughter that had never been any part of his life. I have already transferred the money from the London branch to Eira's account here in Mumbles and wrote her a letter explaining my actions and reasons. Although there has not been a response from her, the bank has assured me the money is now in her account. She and I are all we both really have in terms of family, and her son, of course, and I am hoping that eventually she and I can come to some understanding, and perhaps at least be on speaking terms.

"As for my own financial status, having no one and nothing to have spent my salary on, I have saved all these years. My own account is well endowed. And the estate agent assures me the house in London will sell for more than I could have imagined. With my position at the library, although it won't pay much, I will indeed be fine."

Serena turned to Charlotte and raised her glass. "To Charlotte, a generous and courageous woman. Welcome to your new home. May you find in Mumbles all that brings you peace and happiness." Smiles and salutations accompanied the clinking of crystal glasses.

All eyes turned to Nonna as she brought Drew's birthday dessert to the table, a large tiramisu baked to perfection from long-hoarded ingredients.

Serena placed a pot of steeping tea and cups beside the rich dessert as Granda poured coffee for himself and Drew, adding some milk and a smile to her cup before pouring his own.

Granda raised his coffee cup. "*Pdn bwydd Hapus*, happy birthday, Drew Girl!" Their voices mingled as everyone joined in.

Nonna served the dessert, and as they ate, the talk of presents commenced. Drew felt so grateful and happy. As Sam took hold of her hand under the table, giving it a gentle squeeze, she found herself wondering at Charlotte's exciting new life ahead of her and what her own future might hold.

"Alright now, one more clearing of the table and we'll have Drew open her gifts." Serena and Howard cleared while Naomi gathered all the packages, placing them squarely in front of her granddaughter and giving her shoulders a quick rub as she kissed each cheek.

Drew eyed the array of gifts as everyone took their seats again, wondering which to open first. She decided on the one from her grandparents. Trying to remove the paper with some decorum from around the small rectangular box, she finally succeeded and eagerly lifted off the top. In it lay an iridescent string of perfectly matched cultured pearls. She looked up at Nonna. "These were Mam's, weren't they?"

"Ie, dear girl. Your father gave them to her on their wedding day. She was twenty-one that year, and now they are yours on your own twenty-first."

Drew rose and gave Nonna and Granda warm embraces. "I'll cherish them always."

She sat down and held up her hair. "Sam, would you do the clasp, please?"

Silently, Sam rose and did just that. The pearls lay attractively round her neck, instantly warm and comforting. Next, she reached for Serena's gift. Unfolding the cloth wrapping, she found a beautiful blouse of pale blue silk. "You spoil me, Serena, making all these gorgeous clothes."

"We are building you a wardrobe, Drew, one fit for a young woman as lovely and intelligent as you."

Next, she picked up an unmarked package, and in answer to the question on her face, Charlotte said, "That is my gift to you, Drew."

Wrapped in a vivid blue and yellow scarf, Drew unfolded the silk to reveal a leather-bound edition of her favorite mystery novel, *Murder on the Orient Express*, by Agatha Christie. "Charlotte, this is too kind," said Drew, wrapping the scarf round her neck and tying a side bow. "Thank you so very much. I've never owned a leather-bound edition, much less one of my most-loved mystery!"

Granda had excused himself for a moment to get more wood. Now, opening the door as wide as possible, he squeezed through the doorway with some commotion. Beside him was a motorbike, and he brought it straight into the kitchen.

"A motorbike!" Drew jumped from her chair, still wrapped in her finery, and went directly to the bike. "Granda! Is this really for me?" She threw one long leg over the seat and grabbed the handlebars, thankful she had on trousers. "How did you know I have so wanted one? Now my rides to work and back will be much more efficient, at least, when we have enough petrol again. Think how quickly I can come and go from Swansea! Is there enough petrol to go out first thing in the morning?"

The smile on Howard's face could not have been bigger. "Oh ie, we will do that, Drew Girl. Now, sit back down and finish your gifts while I take this back into the shed."

Drew wanted to sleep in the shed with her new prize. She knew there would not be much sleep for her tonight and who cared?

One last gift was on the table, this one from Sam. It was small and wrapped in brown paper tied with string. She had no idea what it could be. She looked at him, with that smile on his face.

"Go on. Open it. It won't bite you."

Drew smiled as she ripped off the paper and found a copy of *The Book of Rules*, the instruction manual all firemen, brakemen and engine drivers needed to memorize before taking their exams. It looked almost new. "Oh, Sam . . . thank you. I know this means more than you just giving me the book, and that is the best gift you could have chosen for me." She reached to Sam and pulled him into a tight hug.

"I wanted you to know that I do respect your dreams, Drew Girl," he whispered in her ear.

It was now close to eleven, and Drew saw the older folks trying to hide wide yawns. Goodbyes were exchanged, and as Charlotte was leaving, Sam offered to take both her and Serena home in his lorry.

"Serena, can you stay behind a moment? I want to ask you a favor and then I'll be glad to walk you home," said Drew.

"You had better bundle up, Drew Girl, if you are accompanying me home. And I do not want to ride on that motorbike of yours," teased Serena.

"What a wonderful idea!" Drew motioned for Serena to sit back down at the table where Granda and Nonna joined them, wondering what it was their granddaughter would ask.

Once Drew and Granda explained to Serena what was found in the upper room of the vicarage, Drew said, "As I told Granda, the handwriting on some of the papers in the office looked like a woman's. I think Eira knew about her brother's work with the government, actually helped him in gathering whatever information he was passing on to Mr. Sussex. I think she knows more about what happened than she is telling.

"You have known Eira for a long time and must know what she likes to cook. I'd like you to ask her for a recipe, one that you think she will share, and ask her to write it down for you. That will give us a sample of her handwriting."

"Yes, I can do that. She does have an aspic recipe that I have sampled and have wanted to ask her about. I'll stop by her home tomorrow and have her write it out for me. Oh, and Drew, that is clever thinking on your part."

Naomi left the table and returned with Serena's coat. "And I'll walk you home," said Howard, already heading for the door. "It has been quite an eventful evening. Hope you enjoyed your birthday, Drew Girl."

"It was the best ever, and I thank you three for making it so special."

As she and Nonna finished washing the mismatched dishes and stacking them neatly on the shelves, Drew knew she should be tired, but she had never felt more awake, never happier or more grateful. After one last thank you and hug to Nonna, Drew finally settled into bed at midnight with her book from Charlotte. This was definitely a birthday she would hold forever in her memory. She knew, too, that her parents and brother were there with her—that was her gift from them, that they were always and forever with her.

CHAPTER 22

MOTHER AND SON – THURSDAY, 12 DECEMBER

Today was as good as any, thought Drew, deciding to ride her bicycle from her cottage to the home of Eira Hughes. Inside her leather bag, slung across her side, she carried the recipe Eira had written out for Serena. The handwriting appeared identical to the writing on the papers from the vicar's upstairs office. She also carried the sepia-colored photo of Eira and her brother that Charlotte had found in the vicar's night table. It was hard to believe Alred and Eira had once been laughing children.

Drew had never taken notice of the small house she passed on her way to and from the station every day. It was single-level, nondescript and in some need of repair. The white paint was chipped and discolored, and several window shutters hung slightly crooked on their hinges. The unkept front walk and small, weedy garden added to a sense of lonely isolation. Drew walked to the front door and knocked. After many seconds she knocked again, louder this time, knowing by the sound of a radio from somewhere inside that someone was home.

"And what do you want?" demanded the man who finally opened the door. It was Eira's son, Jac. When she saw him that day at the vicarage, she had been so startled that she had taken little notice of his features. Now she observed he was about her own height and build and was approaching middle age. His black hair and clothes were as unkempt as the house. His aura was dark and ragged. This was a man in turmoil.

"My name is Drew Davies. Do you remember when you came to the vicarage wondering if I needed help packing up your uncle's boxes? I was rude to you that day, and I apologize."

"Ie, you were bloody rude. What do you want now?"

"I have something to give your mother, and if she is home, please ask her to come to the door. Or I can come in, if that would be more convenient."

"She isn't home yet. So, you can give me whatever it is you have." As he held out his hand, assuming Drew would give him what she held for his mother, she noticed thin pink lines crisscrossing his palm.

She was becoming less and less tolerant of this man's obtuse behavior. "Actually, I need to speak to her, as well. It's about her brother."

"There's nothin' we want to hear about that old poof. He's dead and gone. And good riddance. My mother has suffered enough because of him so leave her be. There's nothin' you have that she wants."

As he started to close the door on Drew, she quickly put her hand up, stopping it.

"Did you know your uncle well, Jac?"

He turned his coal-black eyes to Drew's with a look of pure fury. "Knew him well enough to hate him, always takin' advantage of my mam and never repaid her and now he's dead and he still owes her plenty. But a dead man pays no debts. Even with him dead, she still gets nothin'."

It was obvious that his mother had not told him of Charlotte's generosity. Attempting to sound sympathetic and keep Jac talking, Drew went on. "It sounds like the situation has caused you a lot of pain. Sometimes, even in families, there are hard feelings. I am sorry."

"Sorry? Why would you be sorry? Nothin' for it now. My hearty thanks to the bloke that done him in. I'll tell my mam you were by." And with that, he closed the door soundly.

Turning to leave, Drew saw Eira just walking through her gate. "Good day, Miss Hughes, I was just speaking to Jac."

"Ie. I heard, and also heard how rude he was. For that I'm sorry to ye. But why are you here, Miss Davies?"

"As I was packing up your brother's belongings, I found something that now belongs to you and thought I would bring it to you rather than stuff it into a box."

"Well, come inside. I don't want to be standing out here conducting personal affairs for all to see," she said, walking past Drew to the door.

Jac was sitting on the couch listening to the radio. "Why are you bringing her in here?"

"Jac, can you give us some time alone? Maybe take a walk or do something useful outside?"

Jac immediately glared from her to Drew, turned off the radio, and stormed out the back door, his dark aura trailing behind him.

Eira let out a long sigh and slowly sat down on the sofa Jac had just vacated, motioning for Drew to sit beside her. "What is it you have for me, young lady?"

Drew found the photograph in her satchel and handed it to Eira. "This was found in your brother's night table, in his prayer missal. They were the only items in the drawer."

Eira hesitantly reached out for the photograph and then, when she took it, laid it in her lap, staring down at the people from a lifetime ago.

After several seconds, Drew realized the sounds filling the quiet room were muffled sobs emanating from Eira. She wondered if the woman was just now realizing her brother was truly gone. Grief washed over her in waves of heart-wrenching sadness.

Drew sat still and allowed Eira to take all the time she needed. After several minutes, Eira reached into the bodice of her dress and pulled out a handkerchief, wiped her eyes several times and blew her nose. She sat still as stone, staring at the photo as she attempted to compose herself.

"Jac wasn't always like this. So rude. So angry. He was a good boy. But he never knew his father, he died before we married, and it has always just been the two of us. I think Jac resents never having known his father and me for never providing one. He joined the army right after school and was away for many years. He was injured in the war and is now back angrier than ever. He won't talk about what happened. He lives in Swansea, but I don't know exactly what he does there. I hardly know him. Even when he visits, it is not easy. The war has ruined so many we care about. Including Alred. I think his death was really about the war."

Drew was more than surprised by Eira's compassionate words and was astonished she was sharing any details of her life. Any time Drew had been around the woman, which had been infrequently, she was always standoffish and distant, holding herself in tight control. Much like her son.

"I am so sorry, Miss Hughes. I'm sure you know that I lost my parents and older brother when I was very young. I often wonder if there is more to what happened to them than anyone is telling. What I do know is that I miss them every day. Loss and grief are extremely hard to deal with. I am truly sorry about your brother and sorry that Jac seems so unsettled."

Eira remained still while Drew spoke. "Thank you, Miss Davies, for bringing this to me," she said finally, dabbing her eyes. "I do appreciate it. And now, I know you must be getting along."

Drew decided to take a gamble, possibly risking her own safety. Could she trust Eira? Or should she fear her? It could so easily turn against her. She chose the former and took her chances. "May I please ask you a question, Miss Hughes?"

"I suppose. What is it?" she said wearily.

"The equipment your brother used to help the military was found in the large upper-floor room of the vicarage. The police have confiscated everything that was there, including the files and ledgers. I believe that you also helped in this work."

Eira's soft demeanor changed instantly. "How did you come by this information? Who are you to have knowledge of this?"

"As you know, the Women's Church Auxiliary gave me the task of boxing up everything in your brother's residence. And, cleaning your brother's home every week, I came to know the house well. Some time ago, I realized there was a false wall where a staircase must be, and although the staircase was hidden, there must have been another way up. I went in and out of the kitchen pantry often when I was cleaning and cooking for the vicar. The day I was packing boxes, I realized there was indeed a stairway to the upper house, in the form of shelves in the pantry built up along one wall.

"My grandfather came back with me and together we climbed that shelf ladder and found the contents of the room. There were two sets of handwriting on the papers and in the ledgers, one your brother's and the other I believe to be yours. I wanted you to know, in case you were approached by the authorities."

"The constables did speak with me. I told them about assisting Alred. He looked through the binoculars, worked the machines, and I wrote. Every week, I took notes for him and made sense of the scattered ones he wrote when I wasn't there. I kept track of what he saw from the window and heard on the wireless. With that information he would fill out the documents he gave to the government man.

"After several years, I wanted him to give up the work. If anyone found out, he would lose his church position, that it would hurt us both. But he said they were paying him good money, that he was saving it. I assumed, because of my helping him for all those years, that part of that money would be mine, but I never saw any of it. Never got a shilling. Never got a thank you, either.

"Did you ever see a man in a suit and bowler hat? Did he meet with your brother?"

"Ie, there was a man like that. I saw him every so often. He'd speak with Alred and take papers away with him. I never learned his name. Alred never wanted me to talk with the man, thinking that even though I helped and knew as much about what went on as he did, he didn't want anyone to know I was involved. Wanted to protect me, he said. Sometimes this frustrated me, because I occasionally came to a different conclusion than he and would document it in a different way. But of course, his opinion dominated, and I just kept my peace.

"I don't think Alred ever told me the entire truth about his activities, and when I questioned him, he'd say I was never to ask about it. That it was his business alone. That is why I think whoever killed my brother wanted to keep him quiet about what he knew, or what they thought he knew. What he was involved with didn't seem earth-shattering to me, as I knew the military must have monitored all ship movements in the channel from the lookouts above, but I wanted him to stop.

He seemed more and more distressed by it all, even after the war ended. I assumed the business was finished, but he continued with it. After the war, I stopped caring about what he did, as we had less and less tolerance for one another." Eira's voice trailed off as she stared across the room, her mind in some different time and space.

"I understand, Miss Hughes. The war held dangers for many people in many ways. Ways we probably can't understand. Ways that change people. Again, I am so sorry for your loss."

Drew became aware that Eira had not heard any of her words and doubted she even realized Drew was in the room. She was but a faceless person.

Suddenly, Eira turned to Drew, her eyes far away and sad. "I came to hate him, you know. Hated everything about him. He was the same man in the end as Jac's father. Both of them with bastard children they never cared anything about. And in the end, he didn't care about me either. He should have left me whatever he had from all that nasty business he got us involved in. But he left nothing, nothing but a wasted life and our ruined reputations. I am not sorry he is gone. He will not be missed."

Drew stood up, knowing it was time to leave and spoke as gently as she could. "Charlotte told me that she put money from your brother's will into your account at the bank, knowing that most of it rightfully belonged to you. Hopefully that will help you some, Miss Hughes. Maybe bring you some atonement as well.

"One last question, please: Why was the false wall in front of the staircase at the vicarage put up, and do you know what year that might have been?"

"It was just after Alred arrived, on about twenty years that would be. The house was always cold and drafty and expensive to heat. He got permission to close up the wall to keep the ground floor warmer. He had no need of the upstairs. At least, not then."

As Drew reached down to put her hand on Eira's shoulder, something on the side table caught her attention. The round end of a shiny blue object was barely visible under a magazine.

Drew left Eira sitting alone on the couch and let herself out the front door. She mounted her bike, catching sight of Jac watching her from the edge of the property. She gave him a wave, and in return he gave her a salute. Drew rode off wondering if Eira's hatred of her brother could have provoked her to murder. Could he have told her that he was leaving what money he had to Charlotte, his bastard daughter, rather than to his faithful sister? What did she have to lose by exacting revenge? Revenge was a powerful motivator and, coupled with feelings of betrayal and rejection, could push someone to spill another's blood, even when the blood was your own.

CHAPTER 23

DARK AURAS – FRIDAY, 13 DECEMBER

The day seemed to go on forever, the hands on the wall clock crawling across the hours. For today's Pasta Friday, Nonna and Serena had invited Sam to join them. His comments at the birthday dinner about wanting to learn pasta making found fertile ground when the two women got wind of Sam's ambition. Tonight was a Pasta Friday he could attend. Of course, Drew knew they did not invite him merely for pasta making but also to further assess his potential as a possible, or in their estimation probable, husband. The thought made her smile as she realized she sometimes wondered the same thing. Well, here's hoping he can hold his own with the three of them. Drew told herself *she* would only be assessing his pasta-making abilities.

Finally, the clock released her from work, and she hastily gathered her belongings into her satchel. Telling Granda goodbye and that she would see him at dinner, she hurried out to her bicycle and home.

Taking her usual route along the Mumbles waterfront, Drew bent her head, peddling hard against the strong wind coming up from the beach to her left. When the wind momentarily subsided, she slowed to watch the silver curls of strong surf and heard what sounded like someone yelling. She stopped to listen and saw a lone person on the sand, pacing back and forth, stopping occasionally to throw and then retrieve something that lodged into a large piece of driftwood. It looked like a knife. The wind suddenly picked up again as darker clouds moved overhead, and hard rain began to fall.

The person on the beach continued to yell, ranting and throwing their arms about. It was hard to see through the veil of cold rain, but Drew thought she recognized Jac. He appeared as angry as the wind and unsettled as the surf. She set her bike down on the verge of the road and decided to walk down to the beach and ask him a few lingering questions. It would only take a matter of minutes and then she'd be off to home.

As Jac caught sight of her, he stood stock still before running over to the driftwood and removing the long knife. "You again! What is it this time?" he yelled loudly. "You need to bugger off!"

"I was on my way home and heard you yelling. I know when I went to your mother's house you were upset about my wanting to talk with her. She shared what a difficult time you have both had, especially regarding your relationship with your uncle. I wondered if that was why you left your uncle's funeral so early."

Jac glared at Drew, not moving an inch. "I said you need to bugger off, girly. It's nothin' to do with you where I was or wasn't." He threw the knife hard again, impaling the waterlogged wood.

"Did you know that our house was broken into the day of your uncle's funeral? Do you know anything about that? Or anything about a blue fountain pen that went missing from my room? And where did you get the scratches on your hands? From a cat maybe?"

Walking slowly over to Drew, Jac suddenly grabbed her roughly by the left arm and pulled her to the log where he had thrown the knife. He forced her down on the log as he pulled the knife from the wood. "Sit there and don't move. You see this knife? I'm very good with it, and if you make any move to leave or run, you'll get to feel its sharp edge. You got that, girly?"

Drew sat on the wet wood, rubbing her arm and not saying anything as she watched Jac from the corner of her eye. The rain was now coming down in freezing sheets, the strong wind biting at her face and hands.

Jac sat down close beside her, grabbed her wrist and began talking almost to himself, hatred boiling out of him. Threatening storm clouds filled his aura as they filled the sky.

"I'd had enough of his pious weakness. Had enough of his always giving us the short end. He wasn't fit to live, to be loved by perfect strangers in his church when he cared nothin' for his own family, his real family. The pain he caused my mam. Rubbing it in her face. And now here you are pushin' your nose into somethin' that ain't none of your business. But it's too late now, isn't it, girly? Ain't on me that you're meddlesome and nosey. You brought this on yourself, and now I have to take care of you too."

Drew tried to stay calm as she looked up the beach and towards the road, trying to think of some way, any way she could escape and run for all she was worth. She knew if she could get away, he would never catch her, but she also knew he could throw the knife a fair distance and that would be the end of it. So, she would stall him.

"Does your mother know you killed her brother? One murder is bad enough. You do realize that committing a second is only going to make things worse for you. Let me help you. We'll go together to the police, and you can turn yourself in. It will go better that way."

"Help? You think I need help? From you? I needed justice, justice for me and Mam. And that's what I had, till you showed up."

Jac sat tossing the knife end-over-end with one hand while keeping the tight hold on Drew's wrist with the other. "Here's what we're going to do, you and me. We're going to walk back to my mam's house, get in my car, and take a nice drive to my place in Swansea. My place ain't bad, you might even like it," he said, now running his hand over Drew's wet head.

"But why did you have to resort to murder, Jac?"

"My uncle was a liar! He made holy vows to follow the rules and then he broke them!"

"The rules? What rules?" Drew stared at the angry sea, not looking at him, hoping he would keep talking.

"That damn bible he was always carrying on about, his holy book of rules. He knew that bastards are an abomination of whores. The Bible says so, and that Charlotte woman is a bastard, and her mother was a whore! Uncle was leaving everything to a bastard rather than to his real family. Mam told me about the money, money he was hiding. You think she didn't care about that? She's the one stayed by his side all her life. She deserved it!

"She told me about the keys in the cat bell, keys that would unlock what was rightfully ours. But the damn keys were fake! But I wager you have the right keys right here in that satchel of yours, and you know what they open. Well, that's what you're going to help me do. Find what's mine."

The sun had set and dusk was fading. Nonna, Serena and Sam found themselves repeatedly looking from the clock to the window, waiting to see Drew walk through the door.

"It's almost dark, and she is always on time for Pasta Friday," said Nonna, beginning to worry.

Sam jumped up from the table. "I'll just take my lorry, Mrs. Davies, and drive along the coast way she always bikes when heading home," he said, relieved that he could go and look for Drew. The weather was abominable, and she could have had an accident anywhere along the way. "We'll be back in no time."

Sam ran to his lorry, his *offer glaw* pulled over his head, got in and drove off towards the water. Between the impending darkness, the ferocious wind, and the deluge of rain, it was difficult to see anything. His windscreen wipers were barely able to keep up.

Driving slowly along the shoreline, he finally caught sight of Drew's bike lying on the side of the road. He stopped the lorry, rolled down the window and surveyed the beach. There on a log, about 15 meters ahead, he could just make out two figures, one he knew was Drew. Her wet copper hair and the satchel lying against her side allowed for no mistake. The other person was not familiar to him. But he realized it was a man when he raised what looked like a long knife in one hand and with the other hand picked up what appeared to be a wide section of Drew's hair, slashing it from her head.

Sam's heart was racing as he slowly backed up the lorry and got out. Crouching low, he moved slowly down to the beach to approach the man from behind, thankful for the wet camouflage of the rain and the darkening day. Thinking he was far enough behind them, he slowly made his way across the sand to where the man still had ahold of Drew. Now if he could just get close enough to tackle him and get him pinned to the ground before he realized what had happened.

"I always did like copper-headed ones," Jac said, raising the knife to roughly cut off another piece of Drew's hair. "And this will give me something to remember you by."

Just as he started to raise the knife again, Jac caught movement on his right side and flung himself up from the log to face Sam.

"Oh God, not another nosey damn bugger. Well, today I get two for one!"

Jac moved menacingly towards Sam, the knife making quick slashing motions, catching Sam's upper arm. Mixing with the rain, blood began to seep through Sam's rain jacket and drip onto the sand.

Ignoring his injury, Sam attempted to gain control of the knife by grabbing Jac's arm, trying at the same time to push the man's legs out from under him, but Jac stood his ground.

The minute Jac had jumped from the log, Drew moved in the other direction and picked up a large length of solid driftwood. Just as Jac sliced Sam's arm and they began to wrestle, Drew landed a hard blow to the back of Jac's head. He staggered, lowering the knife. She raised the heavy wood again and brought it down hard to the side of Jac's head. He dropped to the ground, where he laid still as Sam grabbed the knife.

"Are you alright, Drew? Good work there!"

"I'm fine but you're bleeding!" She took a neck scarf from her soaked satchel and wrapped it tightly round Sam's arm, tying it securely.

"No worries, I'm fine too. Listen, I have a length of rope behind the seat in the lorry. Run and get it while I stay here with . . . who is this person? Do you know him?"

"Ie, I do and will explain once we get him tied up and into the lorry."

Drew ran through the wet sand, sliding and slipping as she climbed up the rain-soaked grade as fast as she could. Relieved to finally be up on the road, her legs trembled as she ran to Sam's lorry, where she quickly found the rope behind the seat.

She half ran, half stumbled her way back down to the beach as the rain and wind continued their assault. She found Jac standing up, staggering slightly with his head bent to his chest. Sam had one of Jac's arms held tightly behind his back, the man's own knife pressed against the middle of his spine. "Tie his hands behind his back, Drew, tight as you can."

Drew held both of Jac's arms behind his back, saying, "One wrong move, Jac, and I'll bash your head again." Still groggy from the first two blows, Jac didn't fight as she secured his wrists tightly. Sam kicked Jac's feet out from under him, dropping him face down in the sand. Jac was now mumbling what sounded like threats, but anything he said was muted by the wind.

"Good! Now I'm going to hand you the rest of the rope. Tie his ankles together and then we'll get him to the lorry. Do you hear that, Jac-whoever-you-are? Now, we move."

Sam pulled the moaning and now cursing man to his feet as they each took a side of him and half pulled, half dragged him up to the road. Once they reached the lorry, Sam lowered the tailgate.

After checking the knots on the ropes, they lifted Jac up onto the bed of the vehicle, closed the tailgate, and Sam and Drew got into the front seat. Both were drenched, shivering and out of breath. Drew knew she was trembling from more than just being wet. She had never been so afraid, never felt so helpless.

Drew sat close to Sam, a hand on his knee to steady herself. "The police station isn't far. When we get there, we'll ring Nonna and Serena and let them know we're alright. Granda should be home by now as well. They must be so worried. The police will want us to make a statement before we leave, and Granda will want to come be with us."

"Fine by me. I hope they have some warm blankets at the station."

"When I ring home, I'll have Nonna send dry clothes for us with Granda."

"That means I'll be wearing your granda's clothes?" asked Sam with a teasing smile.

"Ie, that's what it means, so you better not get them wet again," she answered with a wink. The light banter helped Drew calm herself, and she began to breathe more slowly.

For the moment, all they could do was hold on to the fact that they were alright and focus on getting through what was sure to be long hours before returning home. Knowing that Alred Hughes's killer was literally tied up in knots in the back of Sam's lorry went some way to dispel the shock of what Drew had experienced on the beach. And Eira, that poor woman. So much loss.

After two hours of questions, going over and over with the police Drew's conversation at the house with Jac and then all that had happened on the beach, they were finally allowed to leave. As soon as they arrived back at the warm cottage, Serena bandaged Sam's arm and checked Drew's scalp to be sure there were no cuts.

Nonna nursed them with food and Granda put more wood in the fireplace, both insisting Drew and Sam calm down and eat before they shared what happened. Vesuvi was on Drew's lap, his warm body radiating much more comfort than the blanket about her shoulders. Sometime later, a full meal of *pasta e fagioli* in their stomachs and a glass or two of red wine all around, Drew and Sam finished telling wide-eyed Nonna, head-shaking Serena, and pensive Granda their story.

"There is so much tragedy to this whole sorry affair. Now Eira will be without both her brother and her son," said Nonna.

"And you two could have been victims as well. You were both quick thinking, or it could have ended badly." Those were the first words Granda had spoken, filled with equal parts anger and relief.

"What will happen to Jac now, Granda? And Eira?"

"The due process of the law will take hold of Jac now. He will be charged, go to trial, most likely be found guilty of murder, and spend much, if not all, of the rest of his life in prison. I doubt very much if Eira will be found complicit in Alred's murder. According to Chief Inspector Lewis, when they initially questioned Jac, he adamantly insisted his mother knew nothing of his intent to kill his uncle. Of course, she'll be questioned, but Lewis is doubtful the poor woman had anything to do with it. They called Mara to go sit with her. Hopefully, the women in her life will rally round her in support, and she has the money from Charlotte to ensure her basic needs are met.

"Because of the military and government's secrecy round Alred's activities during wartime, we will most likely never know who he was actually working for. I still believe, in the end, he was ultimately helping Britain, but that may only be my inability to comprehend how one could betray his own country."

They were all silent for some time before Sam laid his arm across Drew's back. "Well, I for one had no idea Drew had such a strong cricket arm and a solid swing. She stopped Jac cold. He'll have a grand headache tomorrow and two good hills on his head."

Having finished with the kitchen cleanup, Serena headed home, and Howard and Naomi moved to the sitting room and were talking quietly together. Sam and Drew were the last ones lingering in the kitchen, both too exhausted to say goodnight and have Sam be on his way home.

"Thank you again, Sam. You cannot imagine my relief at seeing you on that beach. I knew together we could stop him."

"And you, Drew Girl, cannot imagine my relief when you soundly hit the beast in the head. What a grand tale that will be for the ages."

They finally managed the few steps to the kitchen door, where Sam took Drew's hands into his own. "You put yourself in danger today. Please don't ever do that again, Drew Davies. We could have lost you forever." He pulled Drew into a tight embrace.

She lingered in Sam's arms, saying, "It surely wasn't my intent, but I promise to be more careful."

Sam gave Drew a kiss, then left the cottage and climbed into his lorry. Drew watched the lights until they disappeared into the night.

After a long hot bath, Drew was finally warm and had stopped shivering. She took one last look in the mirror to see if she could tell where her hair was cut off by the knife and decided it didn't make any difference. After giving her head a good rubbing with a towel, she donned her warmest nightgown. Nonna had come into her room earlier and placed two hot water bottles under her sheets. Drew slid slowly into the cocoon-like warmth of her bed and laid still for some minutes, her weary body absorbing the heat, not allowing her mind to think on anything but the comfort of it.

As her spirit settled calmly into her body, she propped her pillows up against the headboard and leaned back with a book in hand, thinking over all the harrowing events of the day. She was surprised that after the nightmare of it all she felt so composed. And how relieved she was that Jac was in custody, that she and Sam were safe and unharmed, and that this day was finally over. Thinking of Charlotte and Eira, she wondered if maybe the two women might, after all their loss, eventually find some solace in one another.

With Vesuvi snuggled against her neck, Drew turned off her bedside lamp and wondered what book of rules her parents might have followed and had those rules played a part in their own deaths.

CHAPTER 24

ENDINGS AND BEGINNINGS – THURSDAY, 26 DECEMBER 1946

C hristmas day had been a quiet one at the cottage. Sam and Serena joined Drew and her grandparents for a simple dinner of herb roasted chicken and potatoes with winter carrots. And Serena's bread, of course, always a staple when they were able to pool their rations of flour. Charlotte and Lillian had stopped over for dessert, a traditional loaf cake, but a modified version created out of necessity. It did have a lovely peach drizzle from the canned stores in the cellar.

The next morning, before dawn, Drew lingered in bed. The memory of Christmas brought up a smile. She and Sam had, unknowingly, both made one another small decorations cut from paper. The train engine Drew cut and colored looked like something his young nephew might have made, but Sam seemed thrilled, saying he would add it to his own family's tree one day. Sam in return gave her a much better rendering of a red brake van. She glanced at it now, hung by thread at the corner of the mirror above her dresser. And the small emerald-encrusted brooch he had given her, one that had belonged to his grandmother, lay beside her on the night table.

Covered by the thick down quilt and the furry creature snuggled tight against her, she felt safe and secure. Vesuvi's purring lulled her into a drowsy state of bliss. How thankful she was the crisis in her own small village had been resolved. And, if truth be told, she was proud of her part in the solving of the vicar's murder.

How grateful she was that, during the entire unfolding of the mystery, Granda was there to talk to and discuss all the twists and turns of events. How much more satisfying than just discussing their work-a-day happenings. While the events surrounding the death of the vicar were unfortunate, she also felt a sense of intrigue and excitement at the memory of it all.

She also realized her granda had a much-layered history, that he was not just a man of singular skills but had a past that made her curious to know more. She hoped that little by little she would learn more of the role he played in the wars. She intuitively knew that somewhere in his past there also lay more answers to her family's death, that their accident that night was more than a lone car veering off the familiar road and into death.

Snuggling deeper into the depths of comfort, she put all thoughts of pain aside and decided to think only of the days ahead. She thought of Sam and how they had worked together on the beach. The next time they ventured to London it would be to welcome in the new year, again guests of his kind and loving family. She looked forward to seeing his young nephews and perhaps reading to them in the children's playroom.

As day began to break, Drew thought again of the new vicar. The church council had announced that he would arrive in late March, take up residence in the vicarage, and deliver his first message to his congregation on Easter Sunday. The newspaper reported that he was a young, single clergyman from Ireland. Mumbles would be his first permanent post after a series of short-term placements, filling in for other clergy throughout his home country of Ireland and in Scotland and North Wales.

She hoped that the new man would require some assistance with housekeeping, as she found she missed the job in addition to the extra income.

And perhaps he would bring with him a cat or a dog for company. He would also need to bring a great deal of patience and fortitude to withstand the rigors of the constant attention sure to be thrust upon him by the eager ladies of the Women's Church Auxiliary.

Just before drifting off, Drew decided she would use her mother's Waterford fountain pen, which Eira had returned to her, to write down all the recipes from Nonna and Serena and create her own book of cooking. This last thought made Drew smile as she sank into sleep. Another book of rules, to be passed along from woman to woman across the generations.

AFTERWORD

The Book of Rules is my first foray into the world of mystery writing, specifically cozy mysteries. Because of my interest in history in general, and particularly the time period in which this story takes place, I have written the book from a historical perspective. However, because the story is one of fiction, I have taken artistic liberties in some places to enhance the plot. Please refer to the excellent and informative website below to learn more about the beautiful village of Mumbles, Wales, and its fascinating history. Sincere thanks again to John and Carol Powell, of Mumbles, the co-editors of the A History of Mumbles website and the authors of many of the articles.

https://sites.google.com/site/ahistoryofmumbles/

READER'S GUIDE

1. Drew is determined to become a railway engine driver, a "railroad engineer" as we say in the USA. Although her dream seems unattainable given the male-dominated profession, she continues to hold her intention. Do you or did you have a career passion that seemed unattainable, and how did you deal with it? Did you make it happen? Do you wish you had made different choices?

2. They say every family has its secrets, and Drew is determined to uncover the truth about the death of her family. This need to know serves as the impetus for uncovering the truth regarding the vicar's murder. Have you ever wanted to pursue a mystery in your own family's history, and did you do that?

3. World wars and politics are full of secrets and mysteries. Long after the battles have ended and the peace papers have been signed, the intrigue plays on throughout history. Are you curious about the past or do you find enough intrigue in the present?

4. *The Book of Rules* shines a light on the importance of family, not necessarily a traditional family structure, and the support that can be found in a loving, supportive environment. How was your family structure unique, and what people made a family for you? How did the circumstances and events in your family shape who you are today?

5. Drew and Sam have similar interests, especially in terms of their love for railroading. Do you think they would still be attracted to each other if not for this shared interest? How important do you think it is for couples to share common interests?

6. Rationing during and after the war years in the UK continued until 1949 and was an ever-present consideration in everything people acquired, through ration cards or money. If you and your family had to live under such harsh conditions, restricting your access to food, clothes, fuel, and activities, what would you miss most and why?

7. There is a magical element to *The Book of Rules* shared among the three women: Drew, Naomi, and Serena. We all possess magic; we just don't always realize what it looks and feels like. Do people tell you that you are particularly kind and caring, or exceptionally generous and loving, or incredibly intuitive and wise? These are gifts that not everyone possesses. What magical gift(s) would you like to possess and why?

ACKNOWLEDGMENTS

It is often said that writing a book is a solitary affair, but for me, I find the opposite to be true. All along the way, my characters are clamoring for my attention and impatiently waiting their turn to tell their part of the story.

And then there are all the precious family and friends who wait more patiently than the characters to read the next installment of chapters and either offer sage advice and input or merely offer support and encouragement by telling me it is great writing. An author needs both types of feedback to balance the adventure and journey of writing a book. And I am immensely grateful to everyone who, in the case of *The Book of Rules*, hopped aboard the train with me and made this book such an incredible joy to write.

My daughters, Laura and Taya, are always my first readers and give me great feedback as I begin my first go round of expanding and building on the bones of the story. I thank you both for your kindness, honesty and generosity of your time and expertise.

And thank you to my dear friend, Dominique Dailly. She is the last reader of all my stories before they go off for the very last final edit, and with the eyes of a French eagle, she always finds the hard to spot missing comma or forgotten quotation mark.

My gifted sister, Kathleen Noble, has again created a spectacularly beautiful cover for the book, once more capturing the spirit of the story and the beautiful coastline of South Wales. We spent time together in October of 2021 at her lovely home in Colorado, researching railway engines in service during post-war 1946 in Great Britain, and particularly those that traveled the southern coast of Wales. Once we found what I believed to be images of my vision for the cover, Kathleen began sketching an original watercolor painting to include the other elements of the setting for the story. And voilà, she produced another masterpiece, for which I am grateful and feel so privileged that we can continue to collaborate in our artistic endeavors. Thank you, Dear Sister.

During my extensive research into the state of things in Wales and Europe following World War II, I came across the glorious and informative website, A History of Mumbles. John and Carol Powell, writers and historians and lifelong residents of Mumbles, Wales, have written and accumulated historical accounts of this area in South Wales where my book is set and provided a treasure trove of information. We have e-mailed back and forth over the last two years as they kindly answer my questions and provide me with further insight. They also read over my manuscript and provided input that allows for accuracy of detail and description. My greatest wish is that I can soon pay them a visit and enjoy Mumbles firsthand.

And I am always joined on the journey of writing a new book by my editor extraordinaire and good friend, Sally Carr. She knows me as a writer so well and comes to know my characters as her friends, too, allowing the books to truly shine and the characters to share their stories in the best possible way. Thank you, Dear Sally, we are a great team.

And last but never least, thank you to my wonderful husband, Terry. Your encouragement and support mean the world.

And to all the readers of my stories, I always write with you perched on my shoulder, hoping every book brings you perhaps some nugget of historical insight and takes you on an adventure you are glad you came along with me on. I hope you have enjoyed this first book in The Drew Davvies Railway Mysteries series, and I look forward to traveling the rails with you again soon in the next book.